A Paper Bag For Anna

Charlene Arseneau Reid

Copyright © 2014 by Charlene Arseneau Reid

A Paper Bag For Anna
by Charlene Arseneau Reid

Printed in the United States of America

ISBN 9781629523699

All rights reserved solely by the author. The author guarantees all contents are original and do not infringe upon the legal rights of any other person or work. No part of this book may be reproduced in any form without the permission of the author. The views expressed in this book are not necessarily those of the publisher.

Unless otherwise indicated, Bible quotations are taken from the New International Version (NIV). Copyright © 1973, 1978, 1984, 2011 by Biblica, Inc®.

www.xulonpress.com

Blessings!
Charlie A. Reid

Intro:

"For I know the plans I have for you," declares the LORD, "plans to prosper you and not to harm you, plans to give you hope and a future." Jeremiah 29:11

My Pastor was preaching about God having a plan and a purpose for every person. I sat with my eyes closed and thought of how *I* could possibly have anything to offer because I always felt too weird to be of any use. Suddenly God showed me a vision of myself as a child gathering things in a paper bag–things that had no real significance and yet to me they were treasures. Something that I had forgotten and it made me laugh to myself wondering how a memory like that could be of any use to anyone? Then God laid out before me a book along with the title "A Paper Bag For Anna". I carried it around in my head for many years and finally put it down on paper; sent it to be edited and there it sat in my computer going nowhere. Perhaps it is God's timing that the book is finally coming out and I pray that His plans for this story will be fulfilled.

A little Background:

Dissociative Identity Disorder (DID) formerly known as Multiple Personality Disorder (MPD) is a little known and controversial mental diagnosis. Though it is found in the DSM5 it is still considered to be a rare mental diagnosis. Living with DID, I assure you it is real and has real consequences that often interfere with my daily life. Though DID begins in early childhood as a survival mechanism; later in life it becomes a problem as it is the method of dealing with all situations and can lead to choices and experiences that can be embarrassing and unexplainable. Before my diagnosis (18 years ago) I saw several counselors and therapists but nothing helped.

When I was divinely lead to my current counselor and given the diagnosis I was scared that it meant I was crazy– but as I began to understand what it was and how it worked I began to unravel the troubling occurrences from my past that had left me in pieces. Though as a child it helped me survive insane situations, as an adult it was crippling as it would cause me to "move on" instead of facing difficult situations. It is my opinion that with God healing and wholeness is possible no matter how difficult the circumstances. I continue to move toward that with God's help.

This book is a glimpse into the life of a recent widow, Anna Mercer, and her family as they respond to the loss of Jerry, loving and devoted husband and father, to cancer. Through their 37 years of marriage Jerry protected Anna by keeping her from having to face the truth of her past. Continuing with their strong faith and family traditions, in his absence, Anna and her family must find ways to cope with their new reality.

Dedicated to my husband, Brent Reid, whose unfailing faith has revealed God to me in a very real way: My children Jennifer, Ryan, and Jordon: My sister Cheryl; My Mom and Stepdad, Mother and Father-In-Law, and my family. To Brian Schrock, Connie Stewart and Shirley Pearce - steadfast believers who show the way without fear. Thank you to all who believed in me and encouraged me to publish.

Chapter 1

Hubtown, Nova Scotia—July 5th 2009

Fifty five year old Anna Mercer stood and looked out the window as her mind drifted to a memory as clear as her favorite view out the back window of their home. It had revealed lush green rolling hills, sprinkled with wild flowers in summer; a multicolored patchwork quilt in fall; and a blanket of sparkling white in winter. The beautiful view had continued unmarred for miles, framed by thick woods that added their own distinct dimension. Anna gladly yielded to the warmth it generated, but tears soon followed and spilled down her cheeks. Yet the comfort continued to embrace her—she'd had no time for this welcome indulgence as six months earlier, her husband Jerry had died of cancer and she had just sold their home of thirty-seven years.

The whole family had known about Jerry's cancer for a year before he had died and together had worked to prepare for the inevitable. Jerry had continually encouraged them to live life as the blessing God meant it to be. He had helped them make some of the harder decisions, too – like selling the house.

"Mom, did you hear me?" Anna was startled back to the present by her youngest daughter, Joanna. The baby of the family at thirty-two, she was always concerned about everyone else. She was married to Robert Newcomb, thirty-three, her childhood sweetheart, and a pilot for Air Ways. They had two boys—Jordon, ten and Ryan, eight. Joanna involved herself in everything her "boys" (Robert included) did, plus she remained active in the PTA and on the church social committee.

"Yes, dear, I'm listening," Anna replied, wiping the tears away as she turned from the window.

"Are you sure you'll be all right?" Joanna continued, her dark brown eyes registering the concern in her voice.

"I'll be fine, dear," Anna answered with as much strength as she could muster.

"Ok, I'll call you later. Sarah will drop off the last of your things around four o'clock," Joanna said.

Chapter 1

"Thank you, Joanna," she said, kissing her on the cheek. "I'll be fine, really, dear. I'll talk to you later."

"Okay. I have to run. The boys are out of school in half an hour and Ryan has a dentist's appointment. We'll all come over after supper to lend a hand," Joanna told her as she returned the kiss.

Joanna ran out the door, leaving Anna alone with her thoughts. She looked out the window again trying to retrieve the memory, but without success. The moment had passed and she could only see the shrub fence that ran across the back of her new yard—nothing familiar here.

Gone were the open fields and wooded hills. Now a cedar-stained wooden fence divided her side of the yard from her neighbors on the right and another ran along the left side of the property. A lilac hedge almost hid the mesh fence that closed in the adequate back yard. It featured a stone patio to accommodate a bistro table and chairs as well as a BBQ just outside the French doors. Ground along the length of the back fence was tilled for a garden and the rest formed a good-sized lawn.

The front yard, smaller than the back, featured a rose hedge around its perimeter. The walk from the driveway to the front door ended with a smaller patio that had enough room for a flower pot and a lawn chair or two. A wrought-iron banister and rail closed it in and an awning shielded the whole area. The front yard was divided from the back by a lilac hedge between the garage and left fence.

Inside the garage an entrance to the house opened into a mud/laundry room with a good-sized coat closet. The room served as a separation between the kitchen that encompassed the back left corner of the house from the living room in the front. From the picture window in the living room, you could see the rose bush and watch the world pass by on the sidewalk lining the street out front. An island with a raised counter on one side to serve as a breakfast nook separated the kitchen from the dining area that opened to the backyard through patio doors. A hallway off the dining and living room led to the two bedrooms—one in the front of the house and the other in the back. The bathroom between them ended the hallway.

Anna never thought she would leave the only place she had ever called home. Could she ever imagine life anywhere else? A wave of guilt washed over her as she realized it had only taken six months to move on. Everyone was so proud of her for doing it so quickly. "How strong she is," they said. Her faith in God and His strength had carried her. She knew that, but she alone knew the only real reason she could move on; she could not live in the house without Jerry. Every room, every view, every smell, every nook and cranny spoke to his memory. Their ghosts haunted and tormented her. Her every sense, too, continually harassed her in those familiar surroundings. They provided no comfort.

This new place held no recollection of Jerry. She felt refreshed, looking around, not smothered by memories. Of course, she still grieved, but now she could remember without feeling suffocated.

She shivered. "It's still not going to be easy without you, Jerry. Help me Lord," she whispered.

Anna turned her attention to boxes that needed unpacking and the furniture waiting to be arranged. A hollow feeling crept into her heart and the tears began again. "Oh, Jerry, I miss you. How do I do this without you?" She lamented. *Why not start with a cup tea?* "That's always the best way to begin anything," she'd always said. So now she'd take her own advice.

Anna needed time to become acquainted with her kitchen. Although quaint and clean, it was small. She sighed as she thought of the large kitchen and family table she'd left behind. It had been the center of their home. They had shared many meals and fun times around that homemade, oversized table. She smiled as she remembered. It felt good to smile at the memories and not be overwhelmed by grief.

She unpacked the kettle and set out to find the cups. As she unwrapped her favorite cup, she realized that she'd never need Jerry's favorite. The ache resurfaced. *Come on, Anna, you've got to get a hold of yourself. Make the tea and move on*, she thought, shaking her head and digging out the teapot.

Anna always enjoyed a good cup of tea. Lately she'd discovered a new flavor—multi-berry herbal, bought for just such an occasion. Soon its tantalizing aroma penetrated the memory-empty kitchen. When the tea was properly steeped, she duly carried a cup out to her new patio. *Amazing how a good cup of tea can make you feel so much better*, she mused as she savored its comfort.

When she finished her tea, she went inside to busy herself with unpacking. The afternoon seemed to fly until the phone interrupted her.

"Hello?" she said cheerily.

"Mom, how are you doing? You sound wonderful," Jonathan, the second oldest inquired. She knew that his handsome face would be lit up in a wide grin and his blue

Chapter 1

eyes would be sparkling, because of her good spirits. *He's so much like Jerry*, she thought.

Jonathan, at thirty-six had grown tall and athletic with the same dark brown hair as the rest of the family, but the only one with his father's blue eyes. He had been the child who brought home all the strays and made everyone feel welcome. Every person or animal deserved respect in his eyes. Anna always knew that only a unique person could capture his heart; her name was Darla Thurston. She and Jonathan knew immediately that they were meant for each other and married six months after they met.

Eleven months later, Hannah came along. Now five years old, she acted so much like her Aunt Joanna that it amazed Anna. Talkative and full of life, she always looked out for everyone else. "She's a grandmother already," Jerry used to say. Fourteen months later, they had another girl, Jamie, now four and sensitive like her father.

Jonathan and Darla had decided that two children were enough, so they were as surprised as everyone else by another pregnancy and the newest addition to the family, Trevor, six-and-a-half months old now, had been two weeks old when Jerry died. Jerry had said that he was God's proof that life is meant to be celebrated. So even in the midst of tragedy, came a family blessing.

"Well, I've done some unpacking and had my first cup of tea. So far so good," Anna replied to Jonathan's query.

"I'm glad to hear that, Mom. That first cup of tea is a good start," he said with a smile in his voice. "Unpacking can be tedious so it requires a good attitude to dive in."

They both chuckled and then Jonathan asked, "Has Sarah arrived with the rest of your stuff?"

"Not yet, but I'm sure she'll be here very soon," she replied, checking the time.

"Great! When she gets there, have her call me so I can come and help bring it in. If you've decided where you want some of the bigger pieces placed, I can move them for you while I'm there," Jonathan told her.

"That would be wonderful, Jonathan, thanks. I'll get her to call you. Bye for now."

"I love you, Mom. Bye," he said and hung up.

Anna looked around at the furniture that needed arranging and again thought of their home. When she and Jerry had purchased the house, it was without indoor plumbing and a decrepit barn stood unsteadily beside it. They had slowly made changes and upgrades, tearing out walls, adding plumbing and renovating until the house became their home. The barn proved to be a bigger challenge but not wanting to tear it down they had restored it as well.

By the time they had finished, the main floor of the house boasted two living rooms—one for the family and the other for entertaining guests—a large kitchen with a pantry and with an addition built on a laundry/mudroom to catch all the dirt before it tracked into the house. She smiled as she thought about this because so often the kids were too excited to stop there before they got into the kitchen, making it just another room to clean. At least it had a little bathroom that saved the kids from running into the middle of the house. Later, by necessity, this had to be upgraded with a shower. The second storey had four bedrooms and a full bath. Her family had filled the ample space with love and memories.

Of course, they had also filled it with furniture, making the move to a smaller place more challenging and painful. What would go and what would not? The kids had taken some of the furniture making Anna pleased to know there would still be reminders of their home in the family. The rest she would have to sell but she had wondered how to place monetary value on sentimental pieces. Jonathan had convinced her to sell at auction, and then purchase what she needed for her new place.

She had just redirected her thoughts about what to do next when thirty-six year old Sarah, the eldest of the family, arrived. Jerry had chosen her name carefully. In the Bible Sarai had been the mother of the promise that God had made to Abram when He gave them a son, Isaac. After that God had changed Sarai's name to Sarah. Jerry felt the name Sarah represented the promise that he had made to Anna that she would always be loved and nurtured.

Sarah, a younger version of Anna at five foot one inch with dark brown hair and eyes, was married to a wonderful man, John Mansour, thirty-eight. A Certified General Accountant and devoted husband and father of their two children: Jenna-Marie – "Jen" their fifteen-year-old daughter and Jeffery – "Jeff" their twelve-year-old son.

"Hello, Sarah, Jonathan just called and wants you to call him so he can come over and help with the unloading," Anna told her as they hugged.

"Ok, Mom, I'll give him a call. How are you doing?" Sarah asked as she went to the phone.

"I'm doing well, dear. Had my first cup of tea, and got some unpacking done," she asserted.

Chapter 1

"That's great, Mom," she smiled. Then she was talking to Jonathan.

"Have you thought of where you want things set up?" Sarah asked when she finished her phone conversation.

"Yes, I think I know where everything will go," Anna replied.

The phone rang again. Anna smiled, and thought this had to be Joseph, the only one she hadn't heard from today. She knew that he would not want to miss the excitement. Joseph, Joanna's twin and three minutes older, never let her forget that he was her big brother, even though he was half an inch shorter. He had a pleasant personality and loved to make people laugh. When he met Sandra Barton, his heart was forever hers. They'd been married the previous year on Halloween day–October 31st, 2008. "Fun with a purpose" they'd called it. Everyone was to 'dress-up' and bring a 'treat' for the bride and groom, or they would get a 'trick' played on them. Jerry and Anna had enjoyed watching the last of their children find their life partner and everyone was glad that Jerry was around to see them married. Sandra fit so well with Joseph that Anna found it difficult to imagine he was ever without her.

"Hello, Joseph. How are you dear?" Anna spoke with a smile.

"Now, how did you know it was me?" Joseph asked in mock surprise. "Have I missed the fun?"

"No. Everyone is about to land here and help get this place in order," Anna replied.

"Great, I'll be right there. Imagine a party without me!" he said and hung up to leave.

Jonathan arrived, followed directly by Joseph. Joanna returned soon after with Jordon and Ryan. Everyone pitched in and helped get the furniture set in place and most of the unpacking done. Before they were completely done, Sandra arrived. A loud chorus of welcomes greeted her.

"And we're almost finished – good timing," Joseph teased, greeting her with a hug.

The family's laughter filled Anna's small place and warmed her heart. *This is so wonderful* she thought.

Sandra whispered something in Joseph's ear. He looked at her and, with tears in his eyes, hugged her tighter. Turning to face them all, Joseph cleared his throat and in a loud, clear, authoritative voice said, "We–that is to say, Sandra and I have an announcement to make."

Everyone stopped and looked expectantly at him.

Chapter 1

Joseph and Sandra looked at each other and then blurted out together, "We're pregnant!"

Everyone congratulated them with wild excitement, talking a mile a minute about the due date, what the baby would be and which they hoped it would be.

Anna, filled with joy, silently whispered a prayer: *My cup runneth over....Thank you God for this blessing.* 'It's just another way to show us that life is meant to be celebrated!' She could hear Jerry say. Her breath caught in her throat and tears stung her eyes as she realized that this would be the first grandchild Jerry would not get to hold. But she pushed the thought away because this was cause for celebration – not sadness. Jerry would be proud of her, she thought.

Now, at nearly 8:00 p.m., they decided to stop for a break and order some pizza. How delightful that the first meal in her new place would be shared with most of her family. Anna smiled, thinking how much Jerry had loved entertaining the whole crowd. What a comfort they were. And now the family was growing even larger.

As they ate the pizza around the new dining table and breakfast nook, Sandra shared that she was about three months along and the baby would come in January.

All too soon everyone had to leave. *The saddest part of any visit*, Anna always thought, *was saying goodbye.*

"We're all a phone call away," they chorused, with assurances to stay with her as she adjusted to her new surroundings.

"You're all sweet and I do appreciate the offer, but I'll have to get used to this sooner or later. Thank you all for coming and helping. I love you all," Anna responded.

"I love you's" rang out while they all exited.

As they pulled away in their cars, Anna stood waving through the front window. After they drove out of sight, she turned and something caught her eye. In the shadowy edge of the rose bush, she thought she saw someone. She looked a little closer, but saw nothing, then shrugged and moved away. She decided to have a bath and settle into bed with a book to help her sleep. Of course, she would enjoy a good cup of tea first.

Chapter 2

July 6th, 2009

Her long night finally broke into a morning laden with fresh feelings of sorrow and loneliness. Lord, she prayed, please give me strength to make it through this day. Thank you for the years I had with Jerry and thank you for our wonderful children. Let me be a blessing to them and live my life to please You. Help me find ways today to move on and not feel so lonely. Bless my children, their spouses and my grandchildren. Control my day and bless me as well.

The phone rang as she poured her morning tea. "Good morning!" Anna said.

"Good morning! How was your first night?" Joanna asked.

"Not bad. The night was long, but I made it. Now I only have to make it through another day. The Lord will give me strength," Anna told her.

"Mom, I'm so proud of you! You've been so strong through this whole thing," Joanna said.

"Well, dear, as I said, the Lord gives me strength," Anna replied with a sadness she hoped didn't come through in her voice.

"Mom, I have to run, but I promise I'll check in later to see how you are. I love you," and she hung up.

The beautiful morning seemed to invite Anna outside, so she took her tea to the back patio. As she sat down to do her devotions, she heard lovely singing coming from her neighbor's yard on the other side of her duplex. The song, an old familiar hymn, came easily to her lips as the singer emerged from the hedge.

"Hello, I'm Verna Hughes. Welcome to the neighborhood," she said after they both finished the song.

"Anna Mercer – delighted to meet you, Verna. And thank you – it seems like a lovely place here." She had made her way to the hedge and shook Verna's hand.

"I see you enjoy a good cup of tea," Verna said matter-of-factly. "That's the sign of a good neighbor."

"I just made it. Would you like a cup?" Anna offered.

"Have mine here," Verna said holding up her cup.

"Would you like to come over?" Anna invited.

"Love to – thought you'd never ask," Verna replied as she made her way over.

They settled into a fresh cup of tea and the conversation flowed. It had been six years since Verna's husband of forty years had also died of cancer. Her close-knit family had moved her here and God had sustained her through it all. Her only daughter lived close by, kept constant contact and made regular visits. Her two boys had moved to Alberta in 2007 so she frequently made trips out to visit.

Anna, pleased with her first new friend, made plans to visit Farmer John's Nursery with Verna, who had offered to help Anna get her garden started.

Anna had thought she could never face life without Jerry, but this new friendship promised to ease the pain in ways she never thought possible.

Soon the two were constant companions.

Chapter 3

November 28, 2009

The summer passed swiftly —Thanksgiving and Halloween Joseph and Sandra's first anniversary- had come and gone. Now, near the end of November, the cold weather brought snow and the inevitable sights and sounds of Christmas.

This would be her first Christmas without Jerry and she wondered what it would be like. Although the daily emptiness in her heart had begun to dissipate, the thought of decorating and continuing family traditions without Jerry caused waves of pain that reduced her to tears. However, she knew that her kids would never allow her to skip these important rituals. By now, Jerry would have been busy cleaning and putting away the usual ornaments to make room for the Christmas ones.

Chapter 3

"Lord," she whispered, "You've been faithful to me in these past few months, but this time of year—so special to Jerry and me—is so hard to face without him. Please grant me your peace and the strength I'll need in the next few weeks."

She could not escape—her family would see to that. She wondered, though, if anyone knew about the secret ache this time of year always brought her. Jerry had and he would always handle it. Tears welled up inside her and she didn't try to stop them. "They are God's way of washing our emotions and clearing our minds," Jerry would say. "Let them flow, Anna, let them flow." And he would hold her while the tears did their work. "Thank you, Jerry, for the reminder," she said aloud as the tears edged down her cheeks. She wrapped her arms around herself. "This is so hard, Lord."

Her days never started without Joanna checking in and never ended without one or more "having been in the neighborhood and dropping in." Today proved no exception.

"Hi, Mom," Joanna said. "I was wondering if you wanted to have some of us come over to help you dig out the decorations. We know that it'll be difficult and we thought we could make it a potluck. We could all bring something for supper and . . ."

"Joanna, dear, you don't need to sell me. I love the idea! I was wondering how I was going to get at it without you all. Thank you," Anna responded, silently thanking God for this answer to her prayer and for blessing her with such a wonderful family. "How about everyone comes over around four o'clock? We can eat and then we can put away the everyday stuff and start decorating."

"Great, Mom. We'll be there. We all want to help, but we also don't want to be pushy. Let us know if we're getting in your face."

"Joanna, you're all so wonderful to me and you've all helped me settle in a lot quicker than I ever imagined," Anna said and meant it.

"Ok, Mom. We'll see you tonight then! I love you!"

The day went quickly and by three thirty her company began to arrive. Joanna, Robert and their boys, Jordon & Ryan, arrived first with a pan of lasagna and some fresh garlic bread. The boys joked that they had made the food in their spare time that afternoon.

"If that's the case," said Robert, "I'm not hungry!"

Sarah came next with her husband John packing a Caesar salad. Jenna-Marie and her boyfriend Sydney would bring croutons when they picked Jeffery up after his basketball practice.

Then Joseph and Sandra arrived. Joseph joked, "We'd better start eating quickly because Sandra's hungry." Sandra jabbed him playfully in the ribs. She was looking very pregnant and very happy. She had that radiant glow reserved for expectant mothers.

Jonathan, Darla, their two girls Hannah and Jamie along with baby Trevor—now 10 months old—entered with a whirl of activity. All talking at once, the girls looked for "Jen" and the baby wanted to get down. They brought a pot of spaghetti.

"I helped make the 'scabetti!'" 5-year-old Hannah announced proudly.

Darla rolled her eyes and said, "A very BIG, help!"

Soon Jenna-Marie, Sydney, & Jeffery arrived. Anna looked around and wished she could freeze the moment—together with her family and so blessed.

After the meal, they cleared away the dishes, packed up all the ordinary knick-knacks and brought out the Christmas decorations. Now came the time she both dreaded and looked forward to.

With Christmas music playing in the background, she remembered how Jerry would describe the meaning with a story about each item. He remembered who gave it, when and to whom or from whom and anything special about it! How he stored all this information, she couldn't imagine, but it sure made this annual event enjoyable.

Before they began, Jonathan prayed, "Heavenly Father, it is so good to be with family. We are so grateful for the blessings You have given us. We are thankful for the way that You take care of us. This is a wonderful time of year, Lord, and we so want to celebrate in the true sense with Christ your Son as the very Center of our celebration. Help us not to get caught up in the worldly view. Help us to celebrate the gift of family and friends and remember all this comes from You. God, we are reminded that this has been a year blessed with the arrival of Trevor and the news of another baby on the way, but this still has been a difficult year in the sense of our loss. We are asking You to help us enjoy this Christmas even without our earthly father. Give us the strength to make this a celebration of what we had with him and to remember the blessing he was to us. Help us, bless us and make us a blessing to others. AMEN."

All chorused, "AMEN."

A new artificial pre-lit tree was taken out of the box and stood in the corner of the living room. With the regular knick-knacks removed from shelves, Christmas memories began to fill the house. Anna stood back as the tree was placed, tears stinging her eyes. How she would miss their family tradition of finding just the right tree out in the woods. They would all don warm clothes and walk out to the woods and pick the perfect tree. Jerry would cut it down, until Jonathan and then Joseph, were old enough. Then Jerry shared this honor with them. They would drag it back to the house and set it up in the "family room." With the hot chocolate ready and the popcorn popped, they would string homemade cranberry garlands for the tree. The Christmas music would be playing for the first time since the previous year. Everyone joined in the festivities. As the family grew, the house became fuller and even more joyous. What could match that?

"Mom, are you all right?" Jonathan asked.

"I'm fine, dear—just reminiscing," Anna said.

"Remembering the tree tradition?" someone asked.

"Yes," she replied.

"Remember the year . . . ," one of them began as the conversation continued with much talking and laughing as the tree was finally positioned. Amidst the fragrance of hot chocolate and popcorn, fresh cranberry garlands were draped on the tree. In record time, they sat in the living room. Only the ornaments awaited their opportunity to grace the tree.

As Anna prepared to open the first box of ornaments, she silently prayed, give me strength, Lord.

She removed the first one and unwrapped it. It was the first ornament she and Jerry had hung on their first tree on their first Christmas together thirty-eight years before. She held it up for all to see. Memories flooded her mind, "So many Christmases," she said. The ornament was frosted-white blown glass, made in the shape of a teardrop. Jerry had the words inscribed: "Jerry and Anna Mercer – First of many Christmases – 1971."

"'This is the first and only ornament that we will put on our tree this year, Anna, because every year as God blesses us, He will add to the beauty by adding to our lives. Each year we will be blessed with new decorations and new memories. This is our beginning,'" Anna found herself saying as she remembered Jerry's words.

"And he was so right." Anna continued with her own thoughts. "Our lives were blessed very much. I only have to look at all of you and see the beauty of our lives together. Each of you has become a decoration in our lives and each of

Chapter 3

you brings a unique beauty," she said with pride. Again, she thought how proud Jerry would be of her.

Sarah echoed these thoughts, saying, "Mom that was wonderful. Dad would have been proud of you. We are too."

All agreed. The rest of the evening they took a turn telling the story behind each ornament, as much laughter mingled with the tears. The kids enjoyed the ornament stories—especially the ones about their own.

No one had yet seen the last ornament in the box. Jerry had ordered it as soon as Trevor, their latest grandson, was born. He always did this for the newest member. Jerry had made a point that this little one would have his special ornament, too.

Anna handed the package to Jonathan. "Jonathan, I think you should be the one to open this and bless it."

Jonathan took the package. In an envelope on the box was a handwritten note. It read:

'This is the last ornament that I will buy, but not the last our family will share. The tree gets fuller and more beautiful every year just as our family does. I can only imagine as I write this how hard it's going to be for all of you, but remember that I am always here with you. I love all of you. "Trevor, you are another of God's miracles and another of God's blessings to our family. Your ornament will be the end of an era, but the beginning of a new one. I could not think of a better way to represent that than the symbol of the alpha and omega. You are the sure sign that God wants life to continue. I only regret that I will not see you grow to be the man God has created you to be.'

This is my prayer for you: That you will grow to love Him who gave you life, to honor Him with this life and to be a blessing to your family as they will be to you.'

'God bless you, Trevor.'

'God bless you all. Merry Christmas 2009'

—Granddad, Dad, Jerry

No one spoke, lost in their own thoughts. Finally Jonathan opened the box and took out the ornament. It had an omega symbol in gold with a small pewter alpha in the center. Trevor's name had been uniquely written across the ornament in silver and dated 2009.

As everyone watched, Jonathan picked up Trevor and helped him put the precious ornament on the tree. Tucking

Chapter 3

the note back in the envelope and putting it in the box that held Trevor's ornament, Jonathan noticed a piece of brown paper sticking out of the box. Knowing that his father never did anything without a reason, Jonathan pulled it out and realized it was a brown paper bag, obviously old and worn. He turned to his Mom who was commiserating with Darla about Jerry's thoughtful gift.

"Mom," he said, "what do you suppose this is for?"

Anna looked up and, seeing the brown paper bag, her eyes grew wide with unbelief. "Where did that come from, Jonathan?" she asked.

"I was sort of hoping you could tell me," he said. "It was in the bottom of the box with Trevor's ornament. Knowing Dad, he put it there for a reason."

All eyes rested on the bag and then on Anna as she broke down crying with sobs that made her whole body shake. Darla wrapped her arms around her and everyone closed in for support. They were all confused, not understanding her reaction.

"Mom," Joanna said, "What is it? What's wrong?"

Anna could only shake her head. She excused herself and left them to wait and wonder. No doubt the bag had a special meaning and Anna alone knew it.

She soon regained her composure and returned to the room. "It's late. I think we've all had enough emotional moments for one night. I need to get my thoughts together before I'll know how to share the meaning behind the bag. Suffice it to say for now that Jerry gave me one every year. I'm not used to getting it without him here. He seemed to know that it made me very sad and always knew how to comfort me. Please let me pray about this and I'll share more about it when I'm ready, ok?" Anna spoke with determination.

Everyone knew that they needed to respect her decision and not press the matter. The also knew it would be hard. They never had any secrets in their family, had they?

"You're right, Mom. We're all tired and this has been an emotional night. I think it is time to go home and get some sleep," Sarah said as she came over to hug her.

The next little while was filled up with cleaning and preparing sleepy children for home. Then the house became silent again. Yet the question still played on everyone's mind. "What was the paper bag about and why did it cause their mother so much grief?"

"What do I do now, Jerry?" she asked out loud, watching her family drive away. "I've always had you here to handle

Chapter 3

this for me." She wept and prayed, "Lord, I was taken by surprise and don't know how to handle this. Please, guide me. I need direction."

Chapter 4

December 5th, 2009

A week slipped by and all Anna could think about was the bag and why Jerry would spring it on her like that. *Had he expected me to find it? That's probably what it was. He surely thought I would be the one to remove the ornament from the box and discover the bag. But, on the other hand*, she mused silently, *wouldn't he have guessed that I would give Jonathan the honor of opening his own baby's ornament?*

"Oh, Anna, you're going to drive yourself mad," she chided herself out loud. "No matter how it happened, you have to face it. With my reaction that night, I can't just brush it off. But, where do I begin?" She prayed about it often, trying to figure out how she could explain it. Meanwhile, the children kept their word and did not broach the subject, even though they still called and one or more visited daily.

Joanna picked her up to do some Christmas shopping at the mall with all the female family members. Anna had looked forward to this girls' day out—a welcome distraction. Winter had descended with snow piled up in deep drifts and banks. Anna loved to watch her grandkids play in it, remembering how her own children used to revel in its glories. As you get older, though, the cold becomes less tolerable. Fear of slipping and falling emerges, as does worry of family traveling on compromised roads. No matter—winter still held its attraction. She couldn't imagine living without it.

From the passenger seat, Anna scanned the yard decorations, imagining how they looked at night. No doubt she would find out on their way home.

Joanna chattered all along the way and Anna tried to keep up with her. "I'll drop you off at the doors, Mom, and then go find a place to park," she said as she pulled up to the mall's main entrance. "The others are probably already here. I'll be in as quickly as I can. This place will be a zoo today," she commented as she sped off.

Anna went in and looked around for family before finding a bench to sit on and wait for them. When Joanna came in,

Sarah and Jen accompanied her. Just as they greeted each other, Sandra and Darla approached from the other direction with Hannah and Jamie in tow. Darla explained that the two girls would only be with them for a short while because Jonathan was picking them up to go skating.

Hannah and Jamie soon found gifts for their brother Trevor and their dad. Just as they started to get bored, as if on cue, Darla's cell phone rang. Jonathan was out front to pick them up. Hugs and kisses passed around and the two were gone. Anna didn't do much shopping, but she got many ideas and enjoyed the easy banter between them all. The boy's wives had become as much her daughters as her own.

"How long before we can sit down and eat?" chimed Sandra, making them all laugh. Happy chatter about the baby and pregnancy continued throughout their meal at the food court. The rest of the day flew by with Anna relishing every minute.

By late afternoon, they said their good byes and headed in different directions, each toward home. A light snow was falling as Anna and Joanne left. Just as Anna had hoped, the Christmas lights twinkled everywhere while the radio played carols. Anna sighed in silence. *Thank You for this perfect day, Lord—such a blessing.*

Chapter 4

"Thank-you Joanna," Anna said as they pulled into her driveway. "I enjoyed this day more than you know!"

"Mom, you don't have to thank me—but you're welcome. We love having you with us. Good night and I'll call you in the morning," she said leaning over to hug her. "I love you!"

"I love you, too, and I'll look forward to your call," Anna responded, returning the hug and getting out.

Once inside the house, Anna made a cup of tea to enjoy some down time. Then she carried it to the front room to sit in the chair by the front window and leisurely watch the snow fall and enjoy the neighborhood lights. She turned on the inside tree lights and snuggled in. She had just started to thank God again when her eyes fell on the paper bag.

How did that get there? She wondered. She knew she had tucked it away, in what had proved to be a vain hope of forgetting about it. As she pondered, the phone rang.

"Hello?" she answered.

"Hi Mom just checking in. Are you enjoying the snow falling?" Jonathan knew how much she enjoyed watching it. The two of them had spent many of his childhood hours fascinated by its treasures—not only on the family sofa but also outside coasting, skiing, skating and making snowmen. These happy memories had become even more precious now.

"Yes, dear. I just sat down with a good cup of tea. How was the skating today?"

"Fun. The first half hour or so was challenging with Trevor fidgeting in my back carrier and the two girls unsteady on their feet. Then Trevor fell asleep and Hannah and Jamie met up with some friends. We stayed for almost two hours," he told her. "You'll have to come with us sometime, Mom— you used to love skating," he added.

"Well, you know, I haven't been on skates for years but I think you're right. I would love to go. Perhaps next time," she said, thinking it sounded fun. "I can remember the challenges of trying to juggle you kids when you were all little. I'm so glad we did it—we made many happy memories."

"Yes, I really understand the "fun" of juggling everything to make time for family. You know that I wouldn't trade it for the world," Jonathan said.

"Yes, children are young only once and for such a fleeting time. I'm glad you're making the most of it," she said.

"Well, Mom, I'd better go and join in the "fun" of bedtime. Have a good night. I love you." He was getting ready to hang up when Hannah asked to talk to Nanna. "Mom, Hannah wants to say goodnight," he said.

"Okay, dear, I love you too. I'll say good night so you can go and get bedtime going," she answered and waited for Hannah to speak.

"Hello, Nanna," greeted Hannah— always older than her years (five going on twenty). "It was fun at the mall with you today. I hope you will come skating with us next time. I have to run because Mom is going to holler soon about getting up the stairs or no story. Maybe sometime I could come and stay with you, Nanna. I think that would be fun." She talked and Anna listened. "Dad is always telling us how much fun you were when they were little. I can't wait to see you again. I know that we are not allowed to ask, but did you think about that bag? It's so hard to wait to know about things. Do you have a hard time not knowing secrets, Nanna? I'm sorry. Dad tells me I have to go. I love you." And she was gone.

Anna didn't get a chance to answer even one of her questions.

"I'm sorry, Mom," Jonathan apologized. "Hannah has a way of talking faster than anyone can think."

Anna laughed, "Sometimes she reminds me of Joanna!!"

Jonathan laughed too, "You have a point there." He paused and added, "I'm sorry about her bringing up the bag. I'll talk to her."

Anna smiled, "It's okay Jonathan. I know it must be on everyone's mind. Tell her that I'm working on it and she'll be the first to know when I'm ready. Good night. I love you. Hugs and kisses to all."

"Thanks, Mom, I'll pass that on. Love you too. Good night." And he hung up.

Anna knew that they had discovered the bag for a reason. Even Hannah was concerned. Suddenly, she felt selfish for making everyone wait. She had never kept secrets from her family. Now was the time to explain. Lord, help me, she prayed.

Chapter 5

She turned her eyes to the window, focused on the shimmering night sky and allowed her mind to drift back in time.

Just as she began to explore the past, something outside in the snow caught her eye. What was that? She moved closer to the window to focus on the shadow in the front yard. Was it her imagination, again? No—she soon spotted a little girl hiding in the shadows looking scared. Worse yet, she clearly was not dressed for this cold weather.

"Poor little thing," Anna said.

Anna tried to signal her to come in. She thought knocking on the window might scare her away. Unsuccessful, she donned her coat and boots to make her way out the door onto the sidewalk. She heard sobs emanating from the shadows where she first noticed the girl, so she silently made her approach.

Not wanting to scare her, she said softly, "Are you all right?"

No answer. She moved closer. The girl didn't move so she felt that maybe she hadn't heard her. When she spoke again, the girl bolted.

"Wait!" she said. "I want to help you. You look so cold. Are you lost?"

The girl stopped to answer the woman who had just joined her in the shadows. "I'm not lost," she said, "but I am cold."

Anna continued to move closer as she said, "Would you like to come in? I live right there in that house. I could make you some hot chocolate and we could call someone to come...."

"NO!" shouted the girl. "Please—no phone calls. I would love the hot chocolate, though."

Anna, nervous about not being able to call anyone, nevertheless agreed to take her in and talk about it.

When inside, Anna went to the kitchen and put on the kettle. The little girl sat at the table shivering, her eyes still red from crying. Anna got a blanket and wrapped it around her.

Chapter 5

"Thank you," she said. "It was pretty cold out there."

Anna had a million questions running through her mind but hesitated to ask them for fear of scaring her off. Finally, she decided the best place to start. "What's your name?"

"Annabelle," she said.

"That's my name too!" Anna exclaimed, "but everyone calls me Anna. Do you live around here, Annabelle?"

Annabelle eyed her suspiciously, "Sort of..."

Anna watched her as they settled down at the table with their hot chocolate. "Are you afraid of someone, Annabelle? I would like to help, if you will let me."

Annabelle looked surprised and answered, "You're already helping me. I'm not afraid of you!"

Anna smiled, "I'm glad you're not afraid of me, Annabelle, but I meant someone else. Perhaps the person you were hiding from?"

Annabelle again eyed her with suspicion. "You really want to know?"

Anna looked her in the eye and said, "Yes, I really want to know." She now felt anxious and wondered if she should call the police. She tried to keep the tension out of her voice as she continued to talk. "You were really frightened when I saw you out there. Don't you think that I should let someone know where you are? Someone is probably looking for you."

Annabelle jumped up and with a terror-filled voice cried, "No! You promised! I would never have come in if you hadn't. No one is looking for me!"

Anna, concerned that she was getting in over her head, responded, "Annabelle, there are people who can help you. Please let me get you some help."

Annabelle bolted toward the door, "I should've known! I can't trust anyone!" She ran out the door into the night, discarding her warm blanket onto the kitchen floor.

Anna chased behind her to the doorway. "Annabelle, come back, I'm sorry! I promise I will not call anyone! Please come back."

No reply. Anna returned to the living room, eyes focused outside the picture window into the empty shadows. What should she do? Should she report this? Should she call someone? She dropped, emotionally drained, into her chair and began to pray. "Oh, Lord, what do I do? Please bring her back so I can help her. Please protect her out there in the cold."

Chapter 6

December 6th, 2009

When the phone rang the next morning she woke up, startled to find she'd fallen asleep in her chair. Immediately she remembered why. Would she ever see Annabelle again? The phone continued to beckon her.

"Hello," she answered as cheerfully as she could manage.

"Good morning, Mom! Did you sleep well?" Joanna asked.

"Well, I had a rather fitful night I'm afraid. I really didn't get to bed. I'm still sitting here in my chair," Anna replied.

"What were you doing—reading?" Joanna asked.

"No, I was looking out the window and reminiscing." Anna decided that it would be best not to say anything about Annabelle. "And, I guess I fell asleep."

"You haven't done that for a long time, Mom. What's up?" she queried.

"Nothing really, dear—just trying to sort some things out and I guess I got lost in it."

"So, did you sort anything out?" Joanna hinted.

Anna laughed. "You know me pretty well, Joanna. But no, I'm still working on it. Be patient. I will let you know when I'm ready."

Joanna sighed, "Okay, Mom, but it's not like you to keep us in the dark and we can't help speculating about the possibilities."

Anna felt tears well up and tried to hold them back. *Now what's the matter with you, Anna—you're falling apart again,* she silently chided herself and then said, "I'm sorry, Joanna, I don't mean to keep this from you all, but I really need to figure out how to share it. Please bear with me!"

"I'm sorry, Mom, I didn't mean to upset you! I never have been good at keeping quiet when I should. I'll try not to bring it up again, but we're all concerned about you. We've never seen you this way. You *do* know that we will help you anyway we can, right?" Joanna pleaded.

Chapter 6

"Of course I do! And I know you're all concerned, but I'm fine. I just need to think it through. That's all." Anna assured her.

"Ok, Mom. Subject dropped—for now! But I can't promise it won't come up again!" Joanna emphasized.

"Fair enough!" Anna said.

"So do you want a drive to church?" Joanna asked.

"Oh, yes dear that would be great." She had forgotten it was Sunday and promptly got busy getting ready.

The day was spent with family and went late into the evening. Anna was disappointed that Annabelle did not come back while she sat with her bedtime tea by the window. She whispered a prayer for her before settling in for the night.

Chapter 7

December 7th, 2009

"Good morning Mom. How about coming out with Darla and me to do a little shopping and have lunch at the Café on Main?" Joanna invited.

"Sounds great! I'd love to," Anna answered.

"Great, we'll pick you up in an hour. Love ya!" They both hung up.

Anna turned toward the window and said another prayer for Annabelle. "I hope I get to see her again," she thought aloud.

The glorious sunny day made the snow sparkle like jewels. As Anna inhaled the crisp, fresh air, she sighed, "How beautiful the world is in the winter."

Anna enjoyed the shopping, but mostly she loved the company. Conversation flowed as freely as the laughter.

Chapter 7

Tired by the time they dropped her off in the late afternoon, she thought she might catch a nap before supper. But just after she had nestled into the couch with her favorite blanket and fallen asleep, the doorbell rang.

Still groggy, she made her way over to the door and wondered out loud, "Now who could that be?"

"Special delivery, Ma'me," said the courier agent. "Please sign here."

Anna signed the document and the courier handed her a package. "Merry Christmas!" She said absently as he turned to leave.

"Merry Christmas," he countered.

Anna closed the door and made her way to a kitchen chair. The package, addressed to her, had no return address. Curious, she opened it to find a plain white box. Inside that, neatly folded with a ribbon tied around it, was a *brown paper bag*! She sat and stared at it in amazement.

"What is going on?" she asked herself. "Jerry, did you do this?" She said to the empty room." It couldn't have been Jerry—how could he have known where she would move after he was gone? What on earth is going on? Someone else knows and is playing with me she decided. "This is a cruel joke," she said.

She looked inside the bag. No note. Nothing.

"What do I do, Lord?" she asked out loud. "I haven't even figured this out myself. How could someone else know what's going on? Jerry was the only other person who knew. Did he tell someone? Why? He knew how much this tormented me!"

She sat down and cried, remembering how Jerry would comfort and encourage her. And the tears just kept on flowing until she was numb.

"I'm going crazy," she told herself. "No, I'm just being silly. One of the children must have sent it to remind me that they're still waiting. That was it! Of course." She decided, putting the package away with the paper bag. Feeling a little less shaken but rather perturbed, she went to make some tea.

Later, settled into bed for the night, she remembered Annabelle. Would she return tonight? She decided to bring her book and read in her chair until she couldn't stay awake. *If she sees my light on, she might come back*, she reasoned.

Shortly after midnight, Anna realized she had fallen asleep in her chair again. She then stared out her front window, searching for some movement out in the darkness. Nothing. Just as she got up from her chair, something moved right under her window.

Chapter 7

She went to her door and whispered into the darkness, "Annabelle, is that you? Please come in, I've been waiting for you!"

Annabelle peered timidly around the corner. "You have?" she asked.

"Well, I was hoping to see you again. Please come in—you look frozen!" Anna stepped aside as Annabelle entered.

"I'm all right," she said. "Do you think I could have some more hot chocolate?"

"Certainly," Anna said.

Together at the table again, Anna posed a question. "Why did you run?"

"I was afraid that you would call someone," she replied.

"I assure you I will not do anything that you don't want. But I'm concerned about you. Where are you staying in this cold weather? Don't you have a home? A family? Friends?" Anna caught herself. "I'm sorry, I'm getting carried away. I'm just concerned about you, Little Anna!" she said.

"I like that," Annabelle said.

"That I'm concerned?" Anna asked.

"No—calling me 'Little Anna,'" she replied.

"Oh, yes. Well, it does fit. It seems so strange that you have the same name as me. If you were ever to meet my family. . ."

"NO!" And she started to bolt.

"It's okay, Little Anna. Please—sit and drink your hot chocolate. I only meant that having the same name could be confusing," she explained.

"Okay, Anna. Thank you! I'm sorry I ran," Annabelle said settling back down with her hot chocolate.

"Me, too," Anna told her. "How about you sleep in my guest room tonight?" Nervous about this decision, she still couldn't let her back out into the cold. Would she be safe? Would she see her again? She was getting attached to this little girl.

"Really?" her eyes grew big with delight! "I would really like that! Do you think it would be okay?"

Now Anna looked a little puzzled, "Why wouldn't it be okay?"

Annabelle lowered her voice and leaned forward, "She may not like it!"

"Who?" Anna asked.

"Don't you know?" Annabelle asked with her face wrinkled.

Chapter 7

"No, Little Anna, you've not told me anything about yourself, so how could I know who *she* is." Anna reminded her.

"Oh," Annabelle said plainly, "I forgot."

"Little Anna, if someone is trying to hurt you, I need to know. I can't help you if I don't know how." Anna, nervous once again about this little girl, wondered about her parents. *Lord, I don't know what to do. Help me!* She prayed silently.

"No one can hurt me now," she said. "I'm with you!"

Anna smiled, but felt her stomach tighten and wondered what to do. She thought that after Annabelle— "Little Anna"— fell asleep; she could call someone, but whom? Who would understand? Who would Annabelle trust? What if she called her neighbor, Verna Cleary, she had become such a support, perhaps she would know what to do. But what if she wanted her to call the police? Annabelle would be forced to leave. Why was she so afraid of that? Why not go to the police herself? She would be in big trouble if Annabelle had run away and her parents were frantic. She hadn't heard about a missing child. No one seemed to be looking for her.

Dear God, she prayed, where is her family? What do I do? If only Jerry was here, he'd know what to do, she thought.

"Well, let's get you settled, shall we?" Anna said leading the way to the spare room.

Annabelle followed. "You have a nice home, Anna," she said.

"Thank you, Little Anna! I hope you will be comfortable here tonight. Tomorrow we can talk about what we're going to do, Okay?"

"Okay," she said as she settled into the safe, warm bed.

Chapter 8

December 8th, 2009

Anna woke with a start about 10:00 a.m. and couldn't believe she was still in bed. Heading toward the shower, she prayed out loud, "Good morning, Lord. Please bless my family and my day. Sorry about sleeping so long." Afterward, she made her way to the kitchen to get a cup of tea and settle into her devotional and prayer time. Strange that Joanna had not called. Then she noticed the phone off its cradle. She couldn't remember leaving it off the hook.

Well, that explains why Joanna hasn't called, she thought. As she went to hang it up, she remembered her visitor and stopped. "Annabelle!" she cried and ran to the spare room, but the girl was gone! *Where did Little Anna come from? And where was she always going? Why did she leave without saying goodbye?* So many questions ran through her head.

"Well, that's what you get for sleeping so late," she chided herself out loud. "This whole thing is so strange," she said, shaking her head. She thought about leaving the bed pulled down—just in case Annabelle came back, but how would she explain it? No, she'd better make it up. She could always prepare it again.

In the kitchen as she puzzled about the whole situation, the phone rang. There she is, Anna thought.

"Mom, who in the world have you been talking to? I've been calling for hours!" Joanna sounded upset.

"I'm fine, really. Somehow the phone was off the hook last night. I must have bumped it when I came home," she said, hoping it made more sense to Joanna than to herself. "I just hung it up when I realized you had not called yet."

Joanna didn't sound convinced, but what could she say? "My gracious, Mom, you will have to be more careful. I was worried sick."

"I know and again I'm sorry. I'll be more careful. What are your plans for the day?" she asked, changing the subject. They chatted for a long while and then hung up.

Anna decided to visit with her friend Verna. During the visit, Anna broached the subject of Annabelle. "Verna, have

Chapter 8

you noticed a little girl hanging around or have you heard about any missing children?"

"I've not seen anyone who doesn't belong here," Verna offered, "nor have I heard of any missing children, either. Why do you ask?"

Anna decided that she needed to tell someone about her visitor. "Well," she started, "I have seen this little girl outside in the shadows at night. She seemed really scared and cold. I've asked her to come in for hot chocolate and..."

Verna interrupted her, "Anna, you must be careful. What if the girl is a runaway and you don't report her?"

Instantly, Anna felt a deep regret. She had promised not to tell and here she had. She then changed the subject abruptly saying, "I told her that I was going to get her help, but she ran out."

"If she comes back, you must call the police, Anna!" Verna said sternly.

"I know," Anna said and moved on to talk about shopping and family.

Verna said, "My sons, Jason and Billy, chipped in and sent me an airline ticket to visit them in Winnipeg for Christmas. I'll be leaving tomorrow and won't be back until the sixth of January. I haven't seen my newest granddaughter. I can hardly wait. Of course, I'm also looking forward to seeing the other three, too."

With that, she brought out pictures and began to share about each one. Anna thought about how blessed she was that all her children and grandchildren were nearby. She enjoyed her visit and tea with her friend and wished her safe travels before she headed back home.

The day soon passed and as the evening shadows fell, Anna began to get anxious about her little visitor. *Was she going to return again tonight? Why did she only come around at night? Where did she go during the day? Why had she left without saying anything?*

Anna also hoped that Verna would not see Annabelle before she did and call the police. Verna would be gone tomorrow and that would give Anna a few weeks to figure out what to do without having to answer any questions.

When she'd finished supper and made tea, she settled into her chair with a book. She couldn't read, though, no matter how hard she tried to concentrate. Something Annabelle had said kept nagging her.

"She may not like it," she'd said. "Who was she?" Anna had asked, but Annabelle did not answer. *Who makes Annabelle so afraid?*

Chapter 8

Just as in previous nights, a shadow caught her attention and she welcomed Annabelle back into her home. *What am I doing?* she asked herself. Thinking of Verna next door, Anna hoped she wouldn't notice.

Annabelle, more comfortable with her now, did some exploring through the house. She found the photo albums and plunked down on the couch to look at them. Anna sat beside her and explained the pictures, eventually looking through all of them. They both seemed to enjoy this wonderful time of reminiscing. When they'd finished the last one, Annabelle asked her if she had any more.

"You don't have any of you when you were little?" Annabelle asked.

"No, this is it," she said. It seemed a little odd now, but it had never occurred to her before. She had no pictures of her life before Jerry. She had an album and a scrapbook from Jerry's past but nothing from her own.

"Why not?" Annabelle asked.

"Well, I'm not sure, Little Anna. I must have had some but I don't know where they are. Maybe they got lost in my move." She searched her memory for an alternative answer, but found none. *That had to be it*, she convinced herself. "I'll have to contact the purchasers tomorrow and ask if they found anything left behind. I've heard that people forget things in a move," Anna continued.

Annabelle was not laughing. In fact, she was crying.

"Oh, Honey, what is it? I'm sorry. I've been so insensitive to you. I've been sitting here enjoying my memories and not thinking about you. You must be very lonely without your family or friends." Anna tried to comfort her.

"No. I'm just sad for you!" she said.

Now Anna was surprised. "For me? Why? I have so many happy memories!"

"But you're missing so many," she sobbed.

"Little Anna, I'm not missing anything! I have so many good memories. I'm sure that tomorrow I'll be able to get those albums back," she reassured her.

"Do you really think that, Anna?" she asked.

"Yes, of course I do," Anna said. "Now how about some hot chocolate before you settle into bed?"

"I hope you won't be disappointed," Annabelle said as she followed her out to the kitchen.

What a strange little girl, Anna thought.

Chapter 9

December 9th, 2009.

The next morning Anna found herself alone again, with the phone off the hook and the spare bed still turned down. *Lord, this is just getting so weird. Perhaps it's time to tell Joanna what's happening*, she thought.

As she was putting away the photo albums, Joanna came in.

"Hi, Mom," Joanna said. "Who've you been talking to so late into the night? Or have you bumped the phone off the hook again?"

Anna was about to tell her about the little visitor when Joanna continued.

"You've been on the phone to the wee hours and on again first thing in the

morning. If I didn't know better, I'd think you had a man in your life," Joanna said playfully.

"Joanna!" Anna chided her.

"Just kidding, Mom, but who've you been talking to?" she pressed.

"A friend," she said as she set the last album on the shelf. "Joanna, do you think that some of our albums got left at the house? I seem to be missing some."

Joanna looked at the shelf. "Looks like they're all there to me, Mom."

"Well, I seem to be missing some from my life before your father and me," she said as she headed to the kitchen for tea.

"Mom, you don't have any photo albums before Dad, not that we've ever seen. Shortly before you met Dad, all your stuff got lost in a fire—I believe that's what Dad said. Remember?" she added following her to the kitchen.

"Well, that explains it," she said. "I guess I had forgotten. Sometimes I forget that I had a life before your Dad. He was my life." A wave of pain suddenly gripped her, so she sat down to keep from falling. She felt so lonely and sad.

"You look very tired, Mom. Why don't you come and spend a night with us? Or go visit Jonathan and Darla. Any one of us would love to have you come and spend time with us," Joanna consoled.

"No!" Anna said abruptly, thinking about what would happen to Annabelle if she was not home at night. No, she couldn't leave her alone.

"OK, it was only a suggestion," Joanna said, hurt by her mother's abrupt response.

"Oh, Joanna, I'm so sorry!! I didn't mean it like it sounded. I was just

lost in thought."

"You've been lost in these thoughts for a while now, Mom. We're worried about you. Ever since the night that paper bag was found, you've been withdrawn and distant. You've never shut us out before, Mom. Please let us in so we can help. We know that this has been a difficult year for you, but Mom we're hurting too. You and Daddy always told us that holding things in doesn't help. You made us talk things out so nothing would have any power over us and we would be free. Mom, please, *talk* to me!" Joanna voice choked with tears. "Mom, we need you! Please come back to us!"

"Joanna, I haven't gone anywhere. I'm right here. I'm sorry about all of this. I really am trying to figure it all out." Anna went to Joanna and hugged her as they both cried and held each other.

Lord, help me to figure this out soon, Anna thought. *My family needs me. Annabelle needs me! Help me figure out how I can be there for all of them.*

Later when Joanna left, she reassured her that things would work out soon.

After supper Anna went to sit in her chair to drink her tea and pray. Absently, she picked up her Bible and opened it. She was not sure how long she read, but suddenly she realized that the Scripture was speaking to her. She made careful note of what she was reading: "For whatever is hidden is meant to be disclosed, and whatever is concealed is meant to be brought out into the open (Mark 4:22 NIV)."

It had been a long time since God had spoken to her in her devotions. She had almost missed it, but there it was. She understood that it was meant for her and felt confident that the Lord would reveal its truth. The Lord was going to help her!

"Lord, thank you!" she said. She set the Bible down.

Suddenly she remembered the package that had come just the other day and decided to get it out and see if she could find clues about who sent it. She examined the box, the ribbon and the bag. Nothing. *Where did this come from?*

Chapter 9

Who knows about the bag? As far as Anna knew, no one else knew except her and Jerry.

She went and retrieved the brown bag Jerry had concealed in Trevor's ornament box. Perhaps something would be there. She hadn't thought to look inside.

Opening it, she found a letter and a key The letter came from Jerry and the key looked like one for a safety deposit box.

Anna settled in her chair setting the key and paper bag down, she carefully unfolded the letter, feeling strong emotions welling up inside her, and began to read.

'Dearest Anna:'

'Happy 56th Birthday; Merry Christmas; and Happy 38th Anniversary.'

'You are probably shocked right now because of the bag and this letter. I hope that you are surrounded by our wonderful family as you read this. I hoped you would all be together to continue to make Christmas as special as all the others we've shared.'

'Anna, I know that you will need them with you because of what Christmas means to you. I also knew that I would not be there for you this year. Of all the things that facing death has made me realize, the hardest is that I will let you down for the second time. I'm crying as I write this because I know that you're hurting and I'm not there to help you. That's why I wanted all of you together when you read this.'

Anna could read no farther. "What do you mean 'second time,' Jerry. You've never let me down, EVER." She cried until no more tears came, then fell asleep from sheer exhaustion.

Chapter 10

December 10th, 2009.

The phone startled her awake. She jumped up so fast that she knocked the package, bag, wrapper, key and letter on the floor.

"Hello?" she said.

"Mom? Are you all right?" Jonathan asked.

"What? Oh, yes. Just, uh, napping," she replied. Realizing that once again she'd slept in her chair all night.

"That's been happening a lot. Are you sure you're all right?" Jonathan repeated, obviously concerned.

"Jonathan, dear," Anna said calmly, "I'm old and we old folk do that sometimes."

"Funny, Mom!!" he chuckled. "OK, so you're all right! Well, how would you like to have some company for the night Saturday?"

Anna almost reacted the same as she had with Joanna but she checked herself and said, "I really am fine, I don't need a babysitter."

Jonathan laughed again. "Well, I'm certainly glad to hear that, but Darla and I do. My office Christmas party is Saturday night and we were wondering if Hannah could spend the night with you. We have a sitter coming but Hannah insists on staying with you."

Anna realized that once again she had jumped to conclusions. *You really are making them wonder about you,* she thought. *You need to get back to reality. You've all but pushed your family aside and for what, a child that you know nothing about and a brown paper bag? You need help!* She chided herself and then answered Jonathan, "I would love to have Hannah come for the night. We'll have a great time." She'd already begun to plan their time together.

"That's great, Mom! Hannah will be so excited." Jonathan was beaming over the phone and Anna's heart warmed at the thought. "You'll both have a wonderful time! I'll drop her off around 4:00pm when I go to get the sitter."

"That would be fine. I'm looking forward to it!" Anna hung up.

Chapter 10

She headed for the kitchen to make some tea and remembered that she had left her cup by her chair. When she had the kettle plugged in, she went to retrieve the cup and saw the debris from her abrupt departure to the phone. With Hannah coming, she would have to put it away and get busy planning their time. She tucked them back in the drawer. Then she made a promise to herself: *This needs to be resolved before Christmas.*

"Help me Lord!" she prayed aloud.

Chapter 11

December 12, 2009.

Hannah bubbled over with excitement when she arrived. Jonathan hardly had her in the door before she started talking non-stop about what about they could do together.

Jonathan and Anna laughed and hugged as they listened to her constant chatter. Jonathan did not stay as he had to pick up the baby sitter and get back home. They said good bye. Hannah had already put her overnight stuff in the spare room.

She called out, "Nanna, did you have someone else over for the night?"

Anna, startled that she had forgotten to make the bed since Annabelle's last visit, didn't quite know what to say. "I guess I just forgot to make it," was all she could muster and tried to change that subject before it went any further. "How about we go out and make a snowman? The beautiful new snow on my front lawn is just begging for a snowman. I've been waiting for a special little girl to come and help me make one," she said enthusiastically.

"Yeah!" Hannah said as she pulled her snow pants out of her bag, jabbering on about how they would make the biggest and best one in town.

They made the snowman and then strolled through the neighbourhood assessing everyone else's. They both agreed that theirs was the best, especially since it sported Grampie Jerry's hat and scarf. When they got back to the house, they were both starved. Anna made KD (the family's favourite macaroni) and hot chocolate. Hannah entertained with stories of school and how she had a part in the Christmas concert and hoped that Nannie would be able to come. Anna assured her she wouldn't miss it.

They settled in to watch some TV before Anna tucked Hannah into bed. They said prayers together and read some of the Christmas Story. Anna reminded Hannah that they had to get up in the morning to go to church so she'd better settle down.

Anna sighed as she finally sat in the silence with her cup of tea. She pondered the precious time that she and Hannah had spent together; she had enjoyed it so much. She looked happily at the snowman waving jovially to passersby.

Relaxed and full of joy, she had all but forgotten about Annabelle. Her eyes began to get heavy when she jumped up with a jolt. Beside the snowman stood Annabelle and she was not alone—an older girl stood with her. She looked like a teenager and they both looked cold!

Anna went to the door and called them inside. At first the older girl hesitated, but Annabelle convinced her that it would be all right.

Once inside, they sat down in the dining room with hot chocolates.

"I love your snowman," Annabelle said.

"Thank you! My granddaughter, Hannah, helped me make it. It was really fun." Then Anna remembered that Hannah was asleep in the spare room. She apologized that she did not have a bed for them, but said they were welcome to spend the night; she could make up a bed on the couch...

"That's okay," the older girl spoke, with what Anna thought a hint of sarcasm "you don't have to worry about us."

Chapter 11

"But she does worry about us, don't you Anna?" Annabelle said matter-of-factly.

"Of course I do," Anna answered firmly.

"You don't even know me!" the older girl spoke again.

"Well, I know that you are with Annabelle – "Little Anna" – and that means that you also don't have a place to stay...."

"That's what she calls me – "Little Anna" Annabelle interrupted. "I'm sorry that I didn't introduce you to Annie," she continued.

"Annie?" Anna said in disbelief. "How do you do? It seems odd that you are also an Ann!"

"I guess that means that you still don't know who we are?" Annie said in disgust, standing up to leave.

"Come on, Annie," Annabelle said, "give her a chance."

"Yes, please, give me a chance," Anna pleaded. "I'm so confused. You two obviously know me, but I, well, I really *don't* know you."

"Anna, didn't you read the note?" Annabelle asked.

"The note?" Anna was confused again.

"The one in the bag?" Annabelle said.

"The one in the bag?" Anna asked, still uncertain of what this meant.

"Come on, Annabelle, we don't have time for this." Annie got up to leave again.

"Please!" Anna pleaded. "I really don't understand. Please help me! I want to understand!"

"Anna, get the bag from the drawer and read the letter," Annie said without compassion. "You will understand once you do."

At that moment, the phone rang and startled Anna. She rose to answer it and excused herself. *How does "Annie" know about the letter?* She marvelled.

"Hi, Mom! Everything okay?" It was Jonathan.

"Oh, everything's fine. Hannah is tucked in and sleeping soundly. We had a busy time together. We built a snowman, and went for a walk and had KD and hot chocolate...."

"Mom, slow down! Hannah has had an effect on you!" Jonathan said and they both chuckled.

"I guess you're right. Anyway, everything is great and we'll see you in church tomorrow. I'm beat and ready to crawl into bed myself!" Anna said, wanting to return to her company.

"Sounds good, Mom. Thank you and have a great sleep. I'll see you tomorrow. Love ya!" he said. "Give Hannah a kiss and hug from me, Mom, Jamie, and Trevor."

Chapter 11

"I will do that! I love you too. Goodnight!" Anna hung up and returned to the dining table. Her guests had left. She wasn't surprised, but a little sad. She looked out the window toward the snowman. No, they were gone. Too tired to fret, she decided to go to bed and hope they would return tomorrow night.

Chapter 12

December 21st, 2009

Another week flew by and Anna thought how quickly the year was being wrapped up with the bustle of activity—Hannah's school concert, that she insisted Nanna Anna needed to attend, Jamie's Pre-school Christmas party, the Sunday School Christmas Concert, shopping, wrapping, visiting…

This time of year is so busy that we hardly have time to enjoy it, Anna thought as she plopped down in her chair, exhausted from another busy day of shopping with Joanna, Sarah and Darla. "What a wonderful time we always have together," she mused out loud.

She just had time for tea before she had to go out again. Joseph and Sandra wanted to take her to their Christmas Dinner Party. She sat down and looked out her window,

Chapter 12

realizing that she'd not had much time even for that lately. As she relaxed, she noticed a familiar movement under her window. She sat up to get a closer look and there was Annabelle. A sense of guilt grabbed her as she realized that she had all but forgotten this little one in her busyness. She went to the door and invited her inside. Annabelle seemed sad and Anna felt she should be shouldering some of the blame.

"I haven't been around for you lately, Annabelle. I'm really sorry!" she confessed as she made Annabelle a hot chocolate. "This time of year is so busy—" she began, but then thought better of making excuses.

"I'm okay, Anna," she said, "but what about you?"

Anna remembered how this strange little girl always seemed to be more concerned about her than about herself. "Why do you ask, Annabelle? You're the one who has been neglected for the past week or more," she said and then repeated her apology.

Annabelle smiled and said, "I'm used to that Anna, but you don't owe me any apologies. You have a wonderful life and family. You are very blessed and I am very happy for you. I'm concerned that you are neglecting yourself!"

Anna frowned and sat down. "Little Anna, why are you concerned about me? Look around you. I have a wonderful home and family. I'm not in need, Dear. You really need to think about what you are going to do. I want to help you! Why won't you tell me where you live or why you won't let me call anyone for you? Please, Annabelle, let me help you."

Just then the phone rang and Anna excused herself to answer it.

"Hi, Mom!" It was Joseph. "We're on your street. See you in a minute."

"I'm ready, dear," she said and hung up. She rushed back to tell Annabelle she had to leave, hoping she could stay and wait for her to come back. She shook her head sadly as she entered the kitchen.

Annabelle was gone—her hot chocolate untouched.

Anna felt another wave of guilt. "God," she prayed, "please look after her and bring her back again."

When she noticed Joseph in the driveway, she left the dishes and ran out the door. They enjoyed a pleasant evening and a scrumptious meal, but Anna couldn't stop thinking about Annabelle. *Where had she gone? She could have stayed and avoided the cold. Maybe she will come back later.*

"Mom," Joseph said, "are you all right? You look exhausted!"

Chapter 12

Both he and Sandra looked so concerned that Anna felt foolish. "I'm sorry!" she said. "I guess I am rather tired. But this is all so lovely and I'm very pleased that you wanted me to come with you!"

"We're going to take you home!" Sandra said. "We should have thought about how busy you've been lately. We were selfish, really!"

"She's right, Mom. Come on, let's get you home. We'll all be together at the Christmas Eve Service in a couple of days," Joseph said as he stood up from the table.

Anna agreed. "I am tired, but, I'm not about to ruin your night out. Sit down, Joseph. I'm going to call a cab. I'm so flattered that you would both want to spend time with me. I love you both! Now let me get home so I can rest!" Anna said firmly.

She had been shocked to realize that Joseph was right—only a few more days until Christmas Eve! Where had the time gone? She had promised herself that she would deal with the paper bag and what it was all about before Christmas. That would prove more difficult now.

The cab ride home gave her time to think about what she might tell the family. She would explain that Jerry had started a tradition on their very first Christmas. She never really understood the significance, except that somehow it always brought a powerful feeling of loss and sadness. She would cry for a long time while Jerry would hold her. How could she say that to them?

Then there was Annabelle. What if she came back? She decided it was time to discover why she was always out in the cold. Why would no one care about her? And who would make her so afraid?

Chapter 13

Once inside the kitchen, Anna spotted the cup of hot chocolate on the table. Instantly, another wave of guilt swept over her. That poor little thing—how sad that she has no one and I have so many around who love me. And yet, she's always worried about me. *It really doesn't make sense!* She thought.

When the kettle boiled, she made some tea. She had changed into comfy clothes, ready to settle into her chair. I'll sit here in case Annabelle comes back, she thought. On her way, she noticed the open drawer on the phone stand and went to close it. *You're getting forgetful again, Anna*, she chided herself. The open drawer revealed the neglected note and paper bag. Then she remembered the other girl, Annie. She hadn't been with Annabelle the last time.

Goodness, this is so confusing, she thought. *Did Annabelle wonder why I didn't ask about Annie? Well, if she comes back tonight, I'll ask. Maybe she'll come with her.*

Ok, it is time, she told herself. She took everything with her and sat down to read the rest of the letter. She shivered and opened the letter, praying out loud, "Lord, please help me!"

She skimmed the part she'd read and felt tears stinging her eyes. She blinked and forced herself to continue.

"By now, Anna, you know about a little girl named Annabelle."

Anna froze and dropped the letter. *How could he know about Annabelle? She thought. What in the world is happening?* I must be going crazy. Anna felt like the world had sped up and she'd fallen off. Had she really read that?

She was crying again! "What do I do Lord? I need answers. I can't do this alone," she said. A noise outside caught her attention and, feeling relieved, she went to the door to let Annabelle inside.

"You've been crying!" Annabelle said.

Again Annabelle's concern puzzled her. But now Anna had a two questions burning in her mind. Where was Annie? And–How could Jerry know about Annabelle? She needed some answers now.

"Yes, Little Anna, I have been crying," Anna said, trying to compose herself. "It seems that you know a lot about me, but I know nothing about you. Can you please sit down and help me understand? I feel as if I'm going crazy."

"I think you're ready now, Anna," she said as if she was the adult and Anna the child. "You need to let her in, too. It will make more sense with both of us here."

Anna looked at her inquisitively. "You mean Annie? Has she come back with you?"

Annabelle responded, "Anna, please let her inside."

Anna noticed the young lady standing outside, shivering under her window. She went to the door and invited Annie inside.

Annie sat down on the couch beside Annabelle, not saying a word.

"Well, is everyone comfy?" Anna asked, feeling foolish. "Perhaps a hot chocolate is the best way to start," she said, heading toward the kitchen.

"No, Anna, not this time," the newest guest stated. "We just need to get started. Annabelle's right. It is time."

Anna sat back in her chair, gripping the arms as if they could keep her from being pulled into this nightmare. This is the craziest dream I've ever had, Anna thought as she faced her guests. So many questions ran through her mind. *What are you doing, Anna? Why haven't you told your family? What are you going to do now? You're sitting here with two strangers who know more about you than you do. Okay, you've finally crossed over that line. You have gone mad! Go with it, Anna—there's no fighting it now!*

Even as she allowed herself to believe the worst, she felt something familiar stir inside her. She wasn't sure why, but somehow she knew they were not there to hurt her. *Jerry knew the little one. How bad could this be?* She reasoned.

"So where do we begin?" Anna heard herself asking.

"Let us tell you our story," Annabelle said.

Anna's eyebrows shot up as she said, "Yes, I think I would like to hear your stories."

"She didn't say 'stories.' She said 'our story.'" Annie corrected her firmly.

"OK, *your* story." Anna said.

"It's *your* story too, Anna!" Annabelle said.

"You shouldn't be too surprised by that, now, Anna? You must be starting to see the picture," Annie said sarcastically.

Anna looked at her and said, "Annie, with all that's been going on lately, I wouldn't be surprised to find out that my own mother's name was Ann. I feel like I'm in the twilight

Chapter 13

zone here! I feel like I'm losing my mind. Please don't be fooled—I'm not just surprised, I'm in shock!"

"I guess that's fair," Annabelle said.

"Fair?" Annie responded in obvious distaste.

Annabelle just looked at her sadly and choked back her tears. "It doesn't matter anymore, Annie. You know that it's time to move on."

With that, the tears flowed and Anna felt her heart break for this little one. "I'm so sorry that you're hurting, Little Anna. Please, tell me what I can do. Help me understand. You have me at a disadvantage. Both of you know what's going on and I…well…I feel like an idiot. I feel like I should know, but I don't! I really don't. Please, help me to understand," Anna pleaded. "Little Anna, could you please tell our story?"

"Are you sure, Anna?" asked Annabelle.

"Yes, I'm sure," Anna said matter-of-factly.

Chapter 14

"*I* was born in Parisburg, a small town not far from here on Christmas Day 1953."

"1953? How could that be Annabelle – you must be no more than ten?" Anna interrupted.

Annabelle didn't comment, but just continued with the story. "My parents were very poor and alcoholic. They really did not have time for me. Mostly, I was left alone. I pretty much raised myself without their help. I learned how to do a lot of things that kids don't usually learn so young. Mostly, I took care of them and the house. I thought that this was normal. When I started going to school, I began to see the differences between me and other kids. I became very good at making up stories. I even believed them myself. I told everyone that my parents were secret agents. I would say that my real parents would come around when no one else

Chapter 14

would know. Of course, the other kids just thought I was weird. I didn't care. I had too much to do."

"Then, a week away from my tenth birthday, I came home after school and discovered that my house had burned down. Both my parents had been drunk and died in the fire. I was alone. I had no place to go and so I ran and ran and ran. I was cold and tired, hungry and scared. But I had to keep running. I was hoping that my imaginary parents would show up and rescue me. I ran until I couldn't run anymore. Then, I saw an old barn that looked abandoned. It had started to snow and I was really cold. I went inside and found that I wasn't alone. A dog was there mothering her puppies. I went over and played with them until I fell asleep. The hay and the puppies helped me keep me warm. When I woke up, a little boy was looking down at me. I was startled and got up to run."

"'Don't run! It's okay. I won't hurt you,' the boy said. 'My name is Jerry – Jerry Mercer.' He pointed and said, 'I live in the big house up on top of the hill there.'"

"Whoa! Jerry – my Jerry? You knew my Jerry?" Anna felt her head spinning and thought she was going to pass out. This has to be insanity. The thing I've feared all my life has finally happened. Then she remembered what the letter said,

'By now Anna, you would be aware that there is a little girl named Annabelle.'

"Jerry knew you?" Anna heard herself asking incredulously, remembering that she had thought this earlier; she let it sink in for a moment.

"You need to let me finish, Anna. You'll understand better when you see the whole picture," Annabelle pleaded.

Anna nodded and Annabelle continued. "'What's your name?' Jerry asked. 'I don't think I've seen you around here before.'"

"'My name is Annabelle—Annabelle Hampton. And I'm not from around here,' I said bravely."

When Anna heard this little girl use her maiden name, she felt another jolt. She had not thought of that name for how long? Come to think of it, she had never thought of that name since it changed to Mercer when she married Jerry. How strange to hear this little girl speaking it after so long.

"Jerry asked, 'Where are you from?'"

"I told him, 'Parisburg,' not realizing how far I had come."

"He was very surprised and asked, 'How did you get here?'"

Chapter 14

"I told him about my house, my parents and running. Then I started to cry. I wasn't sure why, but I couldn't stop. He came over and put his arm around my shoulder."

"I will never forget what he said to me: 'Let the tears flow, Little Anna. They are God's way of cleansing us. They are God's way of washing our emotions and clearing our minds,' Jerry said, 'Let them flow, Little Anna. Let them flow.' He held me while the tears did their work. He was right. I did feel less sad and able to think more clearly."

Anna well remembered those words and how Jerry would hold her as she cried. *This is one amazing dream*, she decided.

Annabelle didn't stop. "'Thank you, Jerry!' I said."

"He told me that he wanted to take me home. He was sure that his Mom and Dad would let me stay. He told me he had found this dog and brought her here to look after her. When she had the puppies, he helped look after them. He then took me to see some kittens that had been abandoned and left to die and told me how he had also saved them. He fed them and wrapped them in a blanket to keep them warm. They were almost ready to go to other homes by then."

"'Get your stuff and come with me,' Jerry said."

"I went back to the hay mound and picked up my stuff. Everything I had was inside a brown paper bag. He looked at me with so much sadness in his eyes that I almost cried again."

"'Is that all you have?' he asked me. I just nodded." Annabelle was weeping softly.

"Annabelle, you have to continue. We have only a little time left," Annie insisted.

Anna wondered why she was so angry all the time and why Annabelle continued to hang around with her.

Annabelle wiped her tears and began again. "Jerry took me to his house. His parents were really sad to hear about what had happened to me and my family, but they told Jerry that I couldn't stay. They explained that it wasn't the same as bringing home a stray dog or kittens. I was a child and needed a home. There were places for children to go when their parents died."

"I tried to tell them I would be okay without a home, but they wouldn't listen. They called for help."

"That's why you didn't want me to call anybody?" Anna interrupted, suddenly understanding the dismay Little Anna had shown when she had mentioned calling someone for help.

"Yes," Annabelle said and then continued.

Chapter 14

"I got to spend the next few days with his family while Children's Aid decided what to do with me. I had the best Christmas ever. Jerry's Mom and Dad were so wonderful. I thought that my family had really materialized and I was home."

"On Christmas Day, I turned ten and Jerry gave me a present. He had wrapped it in a brown paper bag. I opened it, and inside was a heart made of wood. He had carved it for me. My name was on one side and his on the other. He said that he would always take care of me. He told me that he had wrapped it in the bag so I could see that good things could come in paper bags, too. He told me that his best gift came with a paper bag— me!"

"His parents gave me new clothes and a doll. I had never had new clothes, or my own doll before. They were so good to me." Annabelle paused and started to cry again.

"Annabelle, come on!" Annie pushed.

Annabelle stopped sobbing. "The next day, some people came to take me away. Jerry was so sad when I had to leave. He gave me a note. 'I promise to find you someday and take care of you Annabelle – "Little Anna". Until then, I will pray every day that God will protect you and keep you safe until we can be together again. – Jerry Mercer, December 26,

1963.' I put the note and heart in my paper bag, along with my other treasures."

Anna did not know what to say. How terrible Annabelle must have felt. How sad. She thought about Jerry's promise to find her again someday. That sure sounded like Jerry.

Anna asked gently, "What else was in the bag, Little Anna?"

Annabelle cried again. "It wasn't much, but when I would walk along the road to school and back, sometimes I would find things. They were like treasures to me. One thing was a little rusty key, another was a pretty stone, and another was a locket that had fallen off someone's chain. It had a picture inside of a family. All of them were smiling and happy. I wanted so much to believe that they were my family that I kept it with my other treasures in the paper bag. The paper bag itself was given to me from my father. It was the only thing he ever gave me. I thought it was a wonderful gift, even though he meant it as a cruel joke. It became the only private place I had in the world and the only place I could store my treasures."

"Do you still have them?" Anna asked.

"I don't know," Annabelle said sadly.

Anna said tenderly, "Where do you think they are?"

"I was hoping you would know, Anna." Annabelle answered.

"Me? No, I really don't, Little Anna. I only know that Jerry would give me a paper bag every Christmas and it would make me so sad," Anna explained. "There was never anything in it—just the bag."

Annabelle was crying and Anna did not know what to do.

After a moment she realized that Annabelle was just sitting there looking at her, not saying anything.

"I'm sorry, Little Anna. This must be so hard, but please continue," Anna urged.

"That's the end of my part, Anna." Annabelle stated.

Chapter 15

Annie began, "This is where I come in."

Anna blinked, "Oh? Yes, of course!"

"Yes, so just let me talk," Annie said abruptly. "They couldn't find anyone from my own family to take me, so I was put in foster care. I had clean houses to live in, but no one really loved me. I was labelled 'a problem' because I didn't fit in with any of the other kids, so, I moved a lot. I was about to shipped out again because I was failing in school and didn't really care. Then a group came to our school to perform a Christmas drama and the whole school got to watch. The play was about the birth of Jesus, but it was set in a more modern time and it really touched me, making me cry." Annie paused for a moment to sneer at Anna.

"I wished I could be one of those people in the play. When the play finished, a man came out to talk about what

Chapter 15

the whole drama meant. Then he asked if anyone wanted to come up and pray. I felt so good I wanted to, but I had to wait because of the line-up. People all along the front wanted to pray with us. When it was my turn, I went over to a tall, nice-looking boy. He smiled at me and asked me my name and how he could pray for me."

"Annie Hampton, and I'm not sure how you can pray for me," I answered.

"'Annabelle Hampton?' the boy asked in surprise. 'It's me—Jerry. Jerry Mercer. Remember?'"

"'My name is Annie!' I said abruptly. 'And sure, I remember you. You're the boy who turned me in.'"

"He looked really sad and said, 'If I'd known they would take you away, I wouldn't have done that. But here you are. Maybe we can get to know each other. I don't live far from here. Maybe I could come and visit.'"

"'No thanks!' I cut him off. "I'm not interested in having someone visit me in my foster home. I probably won't be there long anyway.'"

"'Why?' Jerry wanted to know?"

"'Because I'm a problem and I'm failing and, well, I just don't fit in with the other kids.' I told him, not really caring what he thought or how it sounded. Now all I wanted to do was get out of there. This was no place for someone like me. I didn't fit here either."

"'Why don't you stop here, *Annie*?' Jerry asked emphasizing my name. 'Why not show them what you're made of? What happened to that brave little girl who ran so far away and was determined to live on her own?' Then he asked me, 'Do you still have the paper bag?'"

"I was furious and blurted out, 'That's really easy for you to say! Living in a nice home with a great family and having everything else going for you. And I don't carry foolish, childish things around any more!'"

"'Whoa!' Jerry said, 'I'm sorry that you feel that way. And I certainly did not mean to upset you. But you really don't know me, Annie. My parents were killed in a car accident shortly after you were taken. They were doing everything they could to get you to come and live with us. I've been living with relatives ever since. I never forgot you or how brave you were. So, I don't have a great family and I don't have everything I want, but, I never stopped thinking that someday I would meet you again and we'd be able to be together. I never stopped praying for my "Little Anna". I always hoped that the note and heart I gave you would bring you comfort, knowing that somebody cared—really cared. I

Chapter 15

can see that the girl I met has changed and I'm sorry to see the changes.'"

"With that, I walked away furious. And that was the end of Jerry Mercer—until you!"

With that, Annie stopped talking.

Anna waited to be sure that she was not just thinking about what to say next, when Annie added, "So now, you need to fill us in on the rest of our story. How did you meet Jerry again?"

"Wait a second! How old were you, Annie?" Anna asked.

"I was one week from turning fifteen," Annie told her.

"But, Annie I didn't meet Jerry until I was almost eighteen!" Anna pointed out. "That means three years of time are missing!"

"You mean there's another part of our story that none of us knows?" Annabelle said, catching what Anna meant.

"There must be," Anna replied.

"Well, how do we find out?" Annie asked. "I hope you're not looking to me for answers."

Annabelle said, "Anna, what about the letter? Does Jerry mention what happens after meeting Annie?"

"That's a good point, but I haven't read the whole letter yet," Anna confessed. "I had just started when you showed up again, Annabelle. That's why I had been crying."

"Well, we could read it now, right?" Annabelle asked.

"I suppose we could. But I need a tea or hot chocolate or something," Anna said as she got up to go to the kitchen. When she saw the clock, she exclaimed, "It's 3:30 in the morning! I'm not going to be able to continue this tonight. I think we'd better all crash until tomorrow morning. We'll handle this better then, I hope." *And maybe I'll wake up from this nightmare*, she said to herself.

Chapter 16

December 22, 2009

"Mom? Where are you?" Was she dreaming? Or had she really heard a voice calling her. It seemed so far off.

"Mom? Are you here?"

Here? Where is here? Where was she? Struggling to make sense of what she was hearing, Anna tried to move her head toward the sound.

"Mom! Why are you still in bed? It's one o'clock in the afternoon! Your phone is off the hook again and you left your front door unlocked."

Slowly, Anna started to come around. "Joanna? Is that you?" she finally muttered.

"Mom! What is happening? Are you sick? Why are you still in bed? Why didn't you call one of us?" Joanna shot out questions faster than Anna could think.

"Yep, that is definitely you, Joanna," she quipped. "I'm just sleeping in. Is there a crime in that?" Annie asked, still trying to wake up.

"Mom, sleeping in is one thing, but sleeping the whole day away?" Joanna said with concern.

"Okay, okay. . ." Anna pulled herself out of bed and headed to the bathroom. Why don't you put on the kettle so we can have tea after I get freshened up?" she said cheerfully.

"Mom, are you sick? Do you need to go to the doctor? We're worried about you," Joanna said, not content to change the subject.

Gazing at Joanna's face, Anna could see the concern it mirrored and familiar guilt washed over her. *How much longer*, Anna, she thought. *Your family needs to know. You have to tell them something.*

Anna plopped onto the edge of the bed. "Joanna, I know you are all worried about me. But please believe me, I'm not sick and I don't need a doctor." *Well, not a medical doctor, anyway*, she thought. "I'm going to be just fine. Last night I was up a little late working through some stuff."

Chapter 16

"Did you work through it? Is it over? Are you going to let us in?" Joanna interrupted.

"Joanna, please listen. I'm very close to being able to share with all of you, but I'm not quite there yet," Anna restated.

"Well, maybe you need to put it off until after Christmas, so that we can celebrate together," Joanna said with a hopeful tone.

"I'm going to make you promise something," Anna said with conviction. "I want to be left alone until Christmas Eve." Anna rushed on before Joanna could protest. "That's two days away! If I haven't been able to work through this before the Christmas Eve Service, I promise, I will put it behind me until the New Year. But I really want to try and have this sorted out for Christmas," Anna said, desperate for Joanna's understanding. "I think your father wanted it this way."

"Mom, I can't ever imagine Dad wanting you to sort this out on your own. Given the way you reacted that night, it would seem that he wanted us there to help you," Joanna said.

How right she was, Anna thought, as she remembered the letter. But she knew that she had to try to figure this out on her own first. Jerry had always figured everything out for her. Besides, how could she even begin to explain what had been happening lately?

Joanna sighed, "Okay, Mom, I can see that you are trying to figure this out—but only until the Christmas Eve Service at 6:00 p.m. This time of year family must be together—not alone!" she said firmly. Then relaxing, she added, "I'll talk to the others, but after that, you need to let us help you!" Joanna insisted.

"Thank you, dear. I know I'm asking a lot, but I promise time is all I want. If I'm not able to sort it out, we'll all work on it together," Anna agreed. "Now, can I please go to the bathroom and would you please make some tea?"

Joanna sighed, "Okay, Mom—tea it is."

Chapter 17

Anna got out the letter immediately after Joanna left. She hoped she could read it alone before Annabelle or Annie showed up. That is, if . . . She got up and looked into the spare bedroom—empty—just as she had hoped? Or expected?

'By now, Anna, you know about a little girl named Annabelle, and perhaps you have even met another young lady named Annie. Don't let her upset you—she can be gruff, but she has a tender heart I have come to know and to love both Little Anna (that's what I call her) and Annie.'

She closed her eyes for a moment to absorb what she'd read. Jerry knew her visitors long before she did and spoke lovingly about them.

'Little Anna is very caring and worries about everybody except herself.'

Anna had already discovered that. She smiled and continued. But she needs to be loved. She needs to know that she matters, and she needs to be embraced.'

'Annie seems not to care about anyone else, but that's for protection.'

Protection, Anna wondered, *from what? Or whom? Me? Could I be the one she needed protected from? Or was she protecting me? Or Little Anna? That was probably it. But wasn't Annabelle afraid of Annie? Jerry's words seemed clear as mud.*

She continued reading.

'Anna, I feel like such a coward writing this down instead of saying it. It seems selfish now but whenever I brought it up, you would become so withdrawn and sad. Forgive me, Anna! I only wanted you to be happy.'

"But I was, Jerry, I was!" she said aloud, her mind screaming. "How could you think otherwise?"

'I thought I was always going to be there for you and that one day we would be able to talk about this openly. But when you would withdraw, I would miss you so much and finally I vowed never to bring it up again. I hoped it would just be okay. But, one of them would come around and try to talk to you. I would tell her to leave you alone and let you be happy.'

Why would it make me unhappy? Anna wondered.

'And then every year, when the sights and sounds of Christmas began, Little Anna would come around.'

Well that explains Annabelle's timing, Anna thought.

'I would talk to her and we became friends. She wanted to talk to you, too but I would never let her because I wanted you for me. All she really wanted was the paper bag. So every year, I would fold up a plain, brown paper bag, put a ribbon around it, put it in a plain white box, and early in December I would give it to her. This seemed to make her happy and she wouldn't come around again until the next Christmas.'

Okay, so that's what the white box with the paper bag in it was about; but that doesn't explain how the package ended up here. Then it dawned on her, *Of course, I put in a change of address at the post office, so they must have forwarded it to here. Well, that makes sense,* she reasoned.

The letter continued: 'Do you understand the significance, Anna? Do you remember when I first met you?'

"Of course, how could I forget?" she sighed out loud. "You were the most handsome man I'd ever seen. When I woke up, I thought I saw an angel watching over me."

Jerry wrote, 'You were almost ten years old...'

A shock penetrated her body like an electric charge. She read this again to be sure.

'You were almost ten years old...'

Chapter 17

Just as Annabelle had shared the night before.

'...and all you had was a plain paper bag holding everything you owned. I was so impressed and taken with you—a brave young lady and so determined!'

Anna stopped once more to try and absorb this new revelation, surprised that she could still think at all. "Dear God, I know that You are with me and I know You are going to help me through this. Please give me strength. Amen," she prayed silently.

She picked up where she'd left off.

'I loved you from that first moment. Yes, even when you were ten and I was twelve. I found you and told you that I would take care of you. I took you home. My parents said that it didn't work that way. They told me that I would not be able to keep you like the puppy or kittens I always brought home. I didn't understand why. My parents contacted Children's Aid and you were sent to a foster home. But, before you were taken away, we had a few days together and you seemed so happy. My parents thought you were so sweet and wanted to keep you, too. They had to do things the proper way, though. You spent Christmas with us and I gave you your first gift. Do you remember the heart I carved for you? I wrapped it in a paper bag because I wanted you to see that brown paper bags could hold real treasures.'

Anna was hardly able to read because tears blurred her vision. She put the letter down in her lap and let the tears flow, like Jerry had told her, far more times than she had even remembered. Her mind reeled as she tried to understand what it all meant. Finally, the tears stopped and she could read on.

'I made a promise to you the day they took you away. I told you that I would find you again. I wrote you a note and you put it in your paper bag, along with the heart.'

The note read, 'I promise to find you someday and take care of you, Annabelle—Little Anna. Meanwhile, I'll pray every day that God will protect and keep you safe until we can be together again.'

– Jerry Mercer, December 26, 1963.'

Chapter 17

'What you didn't know was that my parents were doing everything they could to get you to come and live with us but, a month after you were taken away, I lost both of them, too. I was devastated and didn't know what to do. As I faced the grief, I always remembered my brave Little Anna. It was you who inspired me to move on. I had to go to live with relatives in New Brunswick. I vowed that, no matter what, I would find you again someday. And as I had promised, I did pray for you every day.'

'Living with relatives is never the same as being with your own parents. You know this better than most, Anna. Even though your parents were not very good, living with strangers must have been very difficult.'

'The relatives were good to me, but I missed my Mom and Dad. They had been pretty exceptional people. Anyway, as I grew older, I became involved with a Christian movement that traveled throughout the area doing dramas and offering people the opportunity to accept Jesus as Saviour. I was asked if I wanted to take my Christmas holiday the year I turned seventeen and tour Nova Scotia. The prospect of sharing my faith with others was exciting enough, but the idea that I might meet you again clinched my decision. The last place I had seen you was in Nova Scotia. I prayed that God would bring you to one of our presentations.'

Okay, so this is where Annie comes in, Anna speculated.

'We had ten places booked and I'd never heard of any of them. We were on our last day and our last presentation before we returned home and I felt very discouraged. I prayed with many people in the long line-up and some accepted Jesus. When a young lady came up to me, I asked her name and how I could pray for her.'

'She told me her name was Annie Hampton! I couldn't believe my ears. There you were in front of me again. You were even more beautiful. I asked if you remembered me. You didn't until I told you my name and asked you about your paper bag.'

Then I saw your face change and I saw hatred. You flew into me about being the one who turned

Chapter 17

you in. My heart ached as I thought of all the things you must have endured to become this angry person. I tried to challenge you to be as brave as you were when you were ten.'

'You spat out about how easy it must have been for me and how childish the bag was and how you had grown up and wanted to be known as Annie. I almost cried, but I still shared with you the truth about what had happened in my life after you were taken. I was so sad to see you this way. But before I could pray with you, you were gone again.'

'My heart sank. I wondered what difference it had made for me to have prayed for you all these years and you had still become so angry. I almost turned my back on faith and gave up praying for you. But when I shared with our leader, he reminded me that sometimes we don't see the fruit of our prayers for a long time, if ever. He also reminded me that you had not known a lot of what had happened after you'd gone from our house. He told me that you needed my prayers more than ever.'

Anna stopped and now wished that Annie was there to tell her that Jerry had not given up on her. Her head began to ache. She realized it was dark outside and she'd not eaten all day. She got up and went to get a sandwich and tea. Sitting down again tea in hand and a hollow ache inside, she wished Jerry could be with her to help her face this.

Then too tired to focus anymore and not seeing any sign of Annabelle or Annie she made her way to bed.

Chapter 18

December 23, 2009.

Waking after a fitful night she was surprised to see that it was almost noon. Tomorrow is Christmas Eve, she said, and I am not sure how I'm going to figure this out. She began with prayers, devotions and her tea. She stared out the window for a while trying to let her mind settle. But it was in so much turmoil. She wished that Verna was home so she would have company for the day to help her have something else to focus on for a brief time. She thought of calling Joanna, but knew that she would then be more determined to help her.

"Jerry," she said aloud, "I am having such a hard time soaking this all in. I really do wish we had had the opportunity to talk about this." Sobs began to shake her as she realized that for the first time ever she felt angry at him. Not sad and missing him but angry that he had not shared this with her while he was alive. She knew that she could reach out to her family but she felt that she needed to face this on her own.

She had been protected from this all her life. She needed to find out if she was as strong as the little ten year old, Annabelle, that ran away determined to make it on her own, or the teenage Annie who held her head high and tried to be strong through all the adversity in her life. Did she, Anna, have what it takes to face this?

She spent the afternoon finishing up last minute shopping, wrapping and preparing dessert for after the Christmas Eve Service. The family always came over and this year was going to be no exception – even if she was not finished with this paper bag business.

It was dark when she finally settled into her chair with the letter and a tea. Before she began to read where she'd left off, she looked outside hoping that Annabelle and Annie had returned. They had. She let them inside and told them about what she'd read, as well as her conversation with Joanna the day before.

Chapter 18

"So we have until tomorrow evening to figure this out. Are you ready?" Anna asked them both with determination.

Annie rolled her eyes and Annabelle said enthusiastically, "Yes, Anna, let's get started."

Anna re-read the part where Annie left Jerry without praying as well as his sad reaction. She paused when she saw Annie crying.

Annie turned her head and said, "Just keep going."

Anna wanted to comfort her, but thought that proceeding with the letter was probably a better choice.

'You told me in our brief encounter that you moved often and were probably going to move again. I promised to pray from that day on that you would be put in a home where they really cared about you. I also prayed that one day I would find you again and look after you personally as I had promised.' I wrote this down in a note and put it in a brown paper bag. I put it in my Bible to remind me daily to pray for you. I still have it in my Bible, Anna. I'm not sure if you have found it or not, but it should still be there. It was dated December 22, 1968.'

Anna set the letter aside to find Jerry's Bible. She had not seen it since she had moved. She looked on the bookshelf and there it was. She took it down and flipped through the pages until she found the paper bag. She took it out and opened it. There was the note. She took it back to her chair and read it.

'I promise to find you someday and take care of you, Annie Hampton, my Little Anna. Until then, I will pray for you every day that God will protect you and place you in a home where they will care about you until we can be together again.'

'– Jerry Mercer, December 22, 1968.'

Now Annie began to sob. "I never knew that he cared about me! I was so mean to him and tried to cause trouble for you, Anna," she confessed.

Annabelle put her arms around her. "It's okay, Annie," she comforted. "Let your tears flow!"

Annie cried until no more tears came and Anna and Annabelle sat with her in silent support.

Anna picking up the letter asked softly, "Shall I continue?"

Annie and Annabelle nodded.

Chapter 18

'When I turned eighteen, I applied as a carpenter's apprentice with a company in Hubtown, Nova Scotia. I figured this was central enough and I could search for you from there. I constantly looked for you everywhere I went.'

"Anna, this must be where you come in." Annie said.

"No, Annie, that's impossible," Anna assured her. "I never met Jerry until he was 20."

"So he is just telling us about the time until he met you?" Annabelle asked "Then where were we?"

"This is where I come in," a voice interrupted. Anna, Annie and Annabelle looked up to see another young lady enter the room.

Chapter 19

All they could do was stare dumbfounded as the latest guest sat down between Annie and Annabelle on the couch.

"I know all of you, but I know you don't know me," she said, holding their attention. "My name is Ann," she stated.

Anna finally found her voice and said, "I guess I'm not really surprised."

"You know the rest of our story, don't you?" Annabelle was excited. "It's nice to meet you, Ann. We were wondering what happened after Annie's part was done. We thought Anna was the last."

"Well, thanks to Annie, I was able to take over and make the changes she wanted." Ann said as Annie looked at her suspiciously.

Chapter 19

"As soon as you walked away from Jerry, the things that he'd said began to register. Do you remember thinking, 'Why can't I stop and turn things around? What happened to the courage I used to have?'" Ann asked Annie.

Annie thought about it and responded, "Yes, I think I do." Then more forcefully she said, "Yes. I do. On my way back to the foster home, I felt really bad about what I'd said to Jerry. I wanted to go back and apologize and tell him how bad I felt about his parents. I really *did* feel bad," she said, trying to convince the others. "Then I stopped and wished I could change and be better." Gaining confidence, she continued, "Here I was fourteen years old (almost fifteen) and so cynical. What had happened to the brave little girl I once was? Why couldn't I stop and make my life here? Why did I have to keep running? That's when I moved aside to let myself change."

She smiled at Ann who then took over. "When I went home, I couldn't sleep that night. Jerry's words kept playing through my mind. Then I remembered the paper bag. I got up out of bed to look for it. I didn't usually take things from my previous places, always wanting to cut ties. I doubted that I had it, but looked through my stuff anyway and found it."

"I knew it!" Annabelle shouted with joy. "You know where my treasures are."

"Let me finish, Annabelle," she said to calm her down and then started again. "I was shocked by my feelings. I took it back to my bed and dumped it out. There were my childish treasures—the rusty key, the pretty stone, the locket with the picture of someone else's family and the note. And inside a smaller paper bag was the little carved heart, with my name on one side and Jerry's on the other."

Annabelle beamed at the mention of her treasure. She had not seen it for so long. Where could it be? She could hardly wait to find out.

"I thought about that note and about Jerry's life after I was taken. I also thought about the play and its message. I had been so angry, I'd forgotten what I had gone up to the front to do—pray. For the first time, I finally cried. As I did, I remembered the words Jerry said to Annabelle. 'Let the tears flow, Little Anna. They are God's way of cleansing us. They are God's way of washing our emotions and clearing our mind. Let them flow Little Anna, let them flow'. I allowed myself to cry until no more tears could fall."

"And he was right—I did feel better and could think more clearly. That night, I made a promise to myself and to

Chapter 19

Jerry: I would stop running and make myself a better person. I would find Jerry again someday and show him that he was right to believe in me. I also decided I would pray for *him* every day."

"I wrote myself a note and placed it along with all the other treasures and Jerry's note back in my paper bag:

'I promise to find *you*, Jerry Mercer, some day and show you that you were right not to give up on me. Until then, I will pray for you everyday that God will protect you and keep you safe until we can be together again. – Ann Hampton, December 22, 1968.'"

"I wanted him to be proud of me. I'd never felt that before in my life. I cared about what he thought and wanted to be a better person. I also hoped that God would hear my prayers since I really didn't even know Him."

"That was the easy part. The next few months proved really challenging. How could I ever turn my grades around or show this family I was worth their trouble? As it turned out, this family had already asked to transfer me."

"In some way, this made it easier to change. I wanted to seem more mature, so I changed my name to Ann. Shortly after my fifteenth birthday I was with new strangers. "

"The family I was sent to lived in a rural area of Nova Scotia. They had three children of their own as well as three other foster kids. I made seven. They also had cows, pigs and chickens and lots of field work. I would learn when spring came that potato fields meant work—hard work."

"From the look on the family's face when I arrived, my reputation had preceded me. But this place would prove far different from any of the others."

"They had lots of rules, not that I wasn't used to those, but rewards came for following them—allowances and trips to town. They even had a TV.

"The thing that made the biggest difference, though, was that this family prayed and went to church! I was amazed that this happened so soon after I began to pray to this God I did not know. I soon found out that He knew me even before I knew Him. The family really felt like a family and they treated us all equally."

"I really liked my new home and felt like I had a family at last. I was old enough to baby-sit and soon the neighbours hired me to watch their kids. My grades improved to the point that I moved to the head of my class. I even had friends. I was being praised for the first time in my life. I was happy and never forgot to pray for Jerry."

"The year I was to graduate, tragedy struck my life again—another fire! The family's home was destroyed. I felt sick, wondering what this meant for me and the other foster kids."

Annabelle gasped and cried out, "The bag? What about the bag? Did it get burned?"

"We got some of our stuff out before the house was completely engulfed," she assured her.

"I was thinking how glad I was that I'd had my bag with me the day my house burned down," Annabelle disclosed.

Ann hugged her and continued, "It was Christmas week and I was turning seventeen. One more year and I could live on my own. I was so devastated."

"The community put together a benefit to help raise money for the family. We all went. I thought they might raise enough to be able to keep us."

"The fundraiser consisted of groups from all around offering their time and talents to help make a successful evening. At the same time, carpenters came and offered their time to help rebuild. Loggers offered to help with the lumber and ladies signed up to provide meals for the workers. Families opened their homes to the family and us. Hope rose in me that I would not have to move again."

"Most of the talent was local, but one of the groups came from Hubtown. The family had a cousin in the group and they wanted to help."

"Jerry Mercer, one of the band members, recognized me as soon as he saw me. I was so afraid that he would not speak to me. But as soon as he saw me, his face lit up and I knew that he had not given up on me. I fell in love with him. When his group finished playing, we went into the back of the hall to talk. "

"'I always knew that I would see you again, *Annie*,' Jerry said with obvious pleasure. "

"'It's Ann, now,' I said politely. 'And I'm very glad to see you again. After the awful way I treated you the last time we met, I'm surprised you would even want to talk to me.'"

"'That's all right. I knew you needed to hear my story so you could stop feeling sorry for yourself and move on. You have, haven't you—moved on?' he asked."

"'I have,'" I answered simply, though I was a little irritated by his presumption."

"'Ah! There now, that's the strong girl I remember,' he chuckled. 'So what brings you here this evening?'"

"'The family that got burnt out was my latest home, so I may be moving on again,' I told him. 'However, much has changed for me, since our last meeting.'"

"'Oh?' he seemed intrigued."

"'Yes, I've turned myself around and now I'm at the top of my class and will graduate with honours—if I'm able to keep up the marks…when…or if…I move. I have also begun to pray—for you, I mean.'"

"'Oh?' he said with surprise that delighted me."

"'Yes, after our last meeting I read the note you had written to "Little Anna" and decided to make a promise of my own— including praying for you. I wanted to show you that I was going to make it and I wanted to see you again.' I watched his face fill with genuine admiration."

"'You've prayed for me? No wonder my life has continued to be so blessed. After I saw you I had almost given up on praying. I resigned myself to face the reality that life is hard and not a fantasy as I had always imagined,' he confided."

"'So you did give up on me?' I asked."

"'Well, let's just say that I became less gullible. But, I never stopped praying for you and hoping to see you again. I find it fascinating how God works. Don't you?' Jerry asked."

"'Yes, He is rather remarkable. How amazing that I discovered Him right when you were questioning Him! My prayers really carried you back to me again?' I said with as much awe as he'd expressed."

"We sat in silence for a while and then Jerry spoke again. 'Where do you think you will go this time?'"

"'I never know. But I do know this: we are destined to meet again. I look forward to that. We will be able to be together soon. I will be able to live on my own in another year and we can find each other,' I said."

"'Well, now that you are older, why don't you contact me when you get settled into your new family?' With that, he wrote down his address and phone number. 'Put this is a safe place—you know where I mean.' He smiled as he placed it in my hand. 'We will be together—you'll see.'"

Chapter 20

Anna, Annie, and Annabelle were soaking in every word, understanding the story unfolding was the missing link between the past and the present. They were anxious to hear the rest and finally discover how Jerry Mercer truly became a part of their life.

Ann continued, matching their enthusiasm. "Within two days of the benefit, I went to my new home in Yarmouth County —seemingly the end of the civilized world. I didn't really go to a home, but became the caretaker of the children in it. I didn't care because I wouldn't live there long. The parents allowed me to attend a church around the corner, but I had to return promptly to look after their children. I soon had all the children attending both church and Sunday school with me. The foster parents were grateful because they could sleep in after having all-night parties. I felt sorry for their kids and wondered what their lives would be like after I was gone."

"You can imagine my difficulty in making new friends and transitioning to a new school in the last half of grade twelve. I barely passed my courses because of all my home responsibilities. Through it all, though, I did graduate—not at the top of my class, and not with friends, but I made it."

"I wrote Jerry several times and wondered why he didn't respond. Then one day in May just before my graduation I found one of my letters in the garbage. I wrote him one last time with the details of the event, inviting him to attend and mailed it myself."

"When the day came, the parents said I couldn't go unless I brought their kids—they were my ticket. So, when we got there, I couldn't sit with the rest of the class. But when the principal called my name, I walked proudly across the stage. Then I heard someone holler my name. I looked out in the crowd and saw Jerry waving wildly and yelling, as handsome as ever. "

"I ran down off the stage and we met in a wonderful embrace, sharing our first kiss. He wanted me to marry him right then, but I had to wait until I was eighteen in December. He drove me and the children home and I invited him in to

Chapter 20

meet the family. My foster parents were drunk and told him to leave. Jerry was appalled by the state of things and told me that I should come with him. I knew it wouldn't work so I told him to go and I would get out as soon as possible. He left reluctantly."

Now Ann was shaking, but she managed to continue. "After he left, I went to get supper ready and suddenly I was grabbed from behind and spun around. A fist ploughed into my face and the father called me names I remembered hearing as a child. He knocked me to the floor and kicked me repeatedly. I wish I had left with you, Jerry, I thought. Then I lost consciousness."

Chapter 21

All eyes were on her waiting. Then slowly it dawned on Anna…

"So, this is where I take over?" Anna queried. "That would be when I woke up in a hospital with a handsome young man standing over me. I couldn't remember anything. I had no idea who I was or where I came from. I was scared."

"The young man said, 'Hi, I'm Jerry—Jerry Mercer. Your name is Anna Hampton and we are engaged.'"

"He came to visit me every day until I recovered enough to go home. He took me to his place and looked after me, helping me walk again—something the doctors did not think would happen. They also thought I would probably not have children. Jerry was so good to me. He did not tell me anything about my life before him, only that my family had been lost in a fire."

Chapter 21

Looking sadly at Annabelle, Anna continued, "I had nothing with me."

Annabelle cried and Anna felt so awful. "I'm so sorry, Annabelle!" she managed.

"On my eighteenth birthday, Christmas Day 1971, we were married. As I walked down the aisle toward him, he was crying. I felt so loved and wondered how I could be so blessed. I never looked back."

Annabelle said sadly, "No, you didn't."

Annie added, "I probably wouldn't have either!"

Ann said, "You never wondered where you'd come from?"

"And how you got to where you were?" Annabelle interjected.

"I never had to look back or remember anything because Jerry protected me," Anna defended herself. "I guess he thought that I would be safer not knowing the past."

"Jerry never forgot any of us," Annabelle said. "But he wanted you to be happy so he kept us from you."

"He wanted to make you feel special. I guess not knowing your past would help you enjoy the future," Annie ventured.

"But a person is not really complete until they can face their past and embrace it as part of themselves," Annabelle stated.

"You were missing out on who you really were, Anna. You didn't know your strength. You didn't know why God became to be so important to you. You didn't understand why you became such a compassionate mother. You just took things for granted," Ann contributed.

"Without knowing the past, you couldn't really live in the present. I guess that I learned that today, too." Annie said.

"Jerry told me he'd known me all his life," Anna said.

"Well, I guess he did," they agreed.

"So, all these years, Jerry had talked to all of you and kept you away from me," Anna said.

"Well, Annabelle and Annie, but not me," Ann interjected. "I posed the greatest threat to your future happiness. Jerry asked me to let you have the life I never could. He wanted you to be happy."

"But, that was all at your expense!" Anna said. "No wonder you hated me, Annie. I must have seemed extremely selfish, never acknowledging your contribution to my life. I'm so sorry—to all of you! Looking back, I know that I wondered about my past and would slip into a dark depression from time to time. But Jerry would be there for me more than ever then, comforting and helping me."

Chapter 21

"Whenever circumstances triggered a past memory, one of us would take over and Jerry learned how to talk to us. He would comfort us to keep us distanced from you," Annie answered.

"Now that Jerry can no longer intervene, you can finally see us," Annabelle said. "When you first saw me," she continued, "I thought you would know me."

"—even though I kept telling her you wouldn't," Annie interrupted, and then apologized.

"Well, now I do know and I think I even understand. But how can I tell my family?" Anna wondered out loud.

"How about reading the letter to them?" Annabelle suggested timidly.

"It couldn't hurt," Ann agreed.

"It won't be easy, no matter what you decide. But you do have to decide," Annie stated.

"Okay, that's what I'll do. I'll read them the letter. After the Christmas Eve Service, we'll all come here and I'll read the letter just as Jerry planned. He always knew the best way to handle a situation. Why should I stop trusting him now?" Anna decided.

"Sounds like a plan," Ann said, with Annie and Annabelle nodding in agreement.

Exhausted, Anna suggested they all get some sleep. Once in her bedroom, she realized the time—6:00 a.m., Christmas Eve morning. When she turned to ask who wanted to sleep in the spare room, they were gone. She tumbled into bed, almost asleep before she remembered the key.

Chapter 22

December 24th, 2009

Bursting with new energy, Anna ran out to the little drawer and pulled out the key. *All right, Jerry, you never do anything without a reason. So what is this for?* She thought. She walked into the kitchen and automatically plugged in the kettle for a necessary cup of tea. "But how am I supposed to know what it means or where it's from?" she mused out loud.

With tea in hand, she went to her chair. There lay the letter. "Of course," she said out loud, "I never did finish reading it. The answer has to be in here."

She found the place where Jerry showed up at the benefit concert after the house fire. Ann had just arrived.

'As soon as I saw you sitting there, I knew you had changed again —this time for the better. You were so beautiful. When you looked at me, I knew you recognized me. I smiled and you smiled back. I felt like you wondered if I was upset with you. I saw the relief on your face when you smiled back. It was really hard to concentrate on the concert but finally, our turn performing ended and I got to talk to you.'

'You told me about your life now and the latest tragedy of the fire. You now anticipated another move and weren't looking forward to it. I wasn't either because I'd finally found you! This time, though, I gave you my address so you could keep in touch. I didn't hear from you until I got your letter in late May. You told me how the new family put your letters in the garbage.

You'd wondered why you'd not heard from me.' 'I arrived just in time to see you walking proudly across the stage. I hollered and, when you saw me, you ran to me. We embraced and shared our first wonderful kiss! I wanted to marry you right then and take you home with me. After the graduation ceremony, I took you and the children home and went inside with you.'

Chapter 22

'Anna, this is going to be so hard for you to hear. I really want you to have someone with you. You need to hear this in a safe place.'

Anna responded out loud, "Oh, Jerry, I'm so glad that you cared about me, but I already know, my Dear. I met Ann and she told me." She spoke as if he was in the room with her.

'I know you think I've always been there for you, Anna, but once I let you down badly. When we went inside the house, the kids teased you about kissing a boy. The parents were drunk and the house looked so untidy. When the father heard them, he became furious; calling you names no person should ever be called. He ordered me to leave and I said I wouldn't leave without you. He tried to sucker punch me, but missed. You told me to leave, assuring me you would get out as soon as possible. I said I wouldn't, but you insisted that it would be better for me to go. You would leave at a better time.'

'I left, Anna. I left Ann there. She was so scared for me. I started driving away but just couldn't continue. I turned around and went back. I couldn't leave you there. I was almost too late, that beast had you on the floor kicking you like you were a dog. I thought you were gone, Anna. I thought that, after all this time of God bringing us together, I had lost you forever.'

As fresh tears rolled down Anna's face, she realized she was no longer alone. Ann, Annabelle and Annie had silently slipped in to listen. They started crying, too, this being the one part of our story none of them knew.

"He loved us, Anna—all of us!" Ann said.

Anna just nodded and went back to the letter.

'All the promises I made to find you and protect you meant nothing. I had let you down.' 'I grabbed him and shoved him away from you. Then he came at me with a vengeance. I yelled for someone to call the police and an ambulance. One of the kids finally moved and ran for help.'

'I was no match for him but, drunk as he was, I fended off his attacks. I had to keep him away from you. It seemed like forever before I finally heard sirens and watched as two burly cops pinned him down. I could finally get to you. You were still breathing, but unconscious. The ambulance arrived and whisked you off to the hospital. I went with you and stayed night and day until you regained consciousness.'

'When you finally opened your eyes I cried. You didn't remember anything! The doctor said this was common and that you would probably recover after a day or so. When you got stronger, the said you would probably never walk again, and worse, that you would probably not have children. You cried so much. All I could do was hold you and promise that I would never let you down again.'

'When you could leave the hospital, I took you home and nursed you back to health. You made a miraculous recovery — no surprise for you, my Little Anna! You amazed the doctors, telling them you recovered because God had sent you such a wonderful guardian angel.'

'On Christmas Day, 1971, we were married! The miracle of watching you walk down the aisle that day made me cry. Afterward, we bought the old house. Then you showed the medical world that God could do even more—you became pregnant with our first baby! One after the other, God has blessed us with children and each proved even more that God wanted to fill our lives to the brim with blessings.'

'I'm so sorry that again I had to leave you, Anna. I'm sorry that I kept you to myself. I particularly wanted to keep you away from Ann. I hope you understand. Do you realize why I couldn't let anyone harm you? I did not want to lose you and couldn't face the truth. But the truth sets us free, Anna. Talk to Annabelle, Anna, Annie and Ann. *Without them, I would never have had you.* So you see how special they are. Get to know them. Embrace them. Love them.'

Anna smiled and whispered through tears, "Thank you, all of you!" The glow on each of their faces said it all. There was no need to thank them.

The letter continued with: 'I need you—Sarah, Jonathan, Joseph, and Joanna—to come alongside your mom right now and support her. But don't do what I did. Don't turn away from Annabelle, Annie, or Ann. They need you, too.'

Chapter 22

'Now I know you're wondering about the key. Well, its for a safety deposit box at our bank. Box #38 PIN 122509. Inside you'll find a special treasure.'

Chapter 23

Annabelle squealed with delight, "My treasure!"

"We don't know for sure what it is, Annabelle," Anna warned.

"Well, she can hope can't she?" Annie said in her defence.

Anna smiled, "I guess anything is possible, but let me finish and see what Jerry has to say."

'I won't be there to give you your gift this Christmas but I hope the bank (As I left instructions) sent the package for Annabelle—her annual paper-bag gift.'

Anna got up suddenly and left the room. She returned with the package she had received earlier in month and handed it to Annabelle. "I know what this is all about now! I wish I had the other to give you – but he didn't forget!"

Chapter 23

Annabelle was delighted with the package and danced around the room hugging it close to her heart.

Anna, Annie and Ann watched her feeling the joy that she was experiencing and revelling in it with her.

Anna soon had to interject with the reminder that time was running out and they hadn't finished the letter.

Everyone settled in to hear the rest.

'I'm going to sign off now and pray that God will allow all this to unfold in His time and with His protection, Anna.' 'Remember that good things can come even in a brown paper bag. After all, I got the most priceless gift with one—you, Anna. I love you with all my heart!

—Jerry, January 5th, 2009'

Saying good bye again was hard. Anna sat there, cherishing the last line.

"Well, what are we waiting for?" Annabelle broke the silence. "Let's go. We have a treasure to find before everything closes."

"Oh dear, you're right. It's ten o'clock Christmas Eve. We have much to do." Anna agreed.

Chapter 24

Christmas Eve 2009

Reflecting Annabelle's school-girl enthusiasm, Anna prepared for the arrival of her beloved family after the Christmas Eve Service. God's Spirit had finally made her whole by exposing her darkened past. When everyone came, they gathered around her chair in eager anticipation.

"Hannah," Anna said, "I promised you would be the first to know when I was ready to talk about the brown paper bag. I'm ready!"

Hannah squealed in delight. Just like Annabelle, Anna thought with a smile.

She picked up the paper bag from the stand beside her. Another paper bag, weather-beaten, worn and obviously full, sat on the floor nearby.

Chapter 24

"I'm going to tell you all about a brave little girl, a feisty teenager and a determined young lady. I'm also going to tell you about another lady who benefited for many years from these three people, never realizing what she owed them. I'm going to share *my* story with you."

Anna began by explaining the strange events that had happened since they discovered the paper bag folded under Trevor's ornament. She told about the strange visits, the special delivery, as well as the letter and key she finally noticed inside the bag.

Reading from the letter and sharing the visitors' stories, she discussed her buried past. Jerry had tried to do what he thought best for her and, when he could no longer hide the truth, he told Anna. She explained that she could finally embrace her past and be her true self for the first time ever. Many tears followed her shocking disclosures, convincing Anna she was right to face this on her own first. *Jerry would be proud*, she thought.

Then, when the conversation waned, Hannah said, "But, what about the key, Nanna?"

Anna smiled thinking, *I know who she takes after now!* "Well, I saved the best for last," she said, rekindling the anticipation.

"I took the key to the bank today and, using the Safety Deposit number and PIN that Jerry included in the letter, I gained access to it. Inside, I found this bag," she said, pointing to the full bag on the floor.

"Is that Annabelle's treasure?" Hannah wanted to know.

Without a word, Anna dumped the contents on the floor. Everyone studied different items, marvelling at the story behind each one — the old rusty key, the pretty stone and the locket. The family in the locket looked more like an image from an old magazine. It also held two notes — one from Jerry to Annabelle and one from Annie. The small paper bag inside held the wooden heart carved with "Annabelle Hampton" written on one side and "Jerry Mercer" written on the other.

As she watched her family pass around the treasures and talk about the story behind each one, she thought about the moment when she'd opened the box with the bag inside. As if a barrier had been lifted, she saw her whole life – not as Annabelle's or Annie's or even Ann's part — but as hers. *She* was that brave little girl, the rebellious teenager and the

Chapter 24

young lady beaten almost to death. She was Anna who woke up in the hospital and was greeted by her angel. She was Anna and this was *her* paper bag. She cried and held the bag close to her heart as she imagined Annabelle saying, "Thank you, Jerry. I knew I would have my treasure back someday!"

Chapter 25

December 25, 2009.

When everyone quieted down, someone noticed the time—ten minutes past midnight, Christmas 2009. Hugs, kisses and blessings were shared. Anna knew that Jerry had planned this moment. Then suddenly, Sarah came in from the kitchen carrying a birthday cake and everyone joined in singing "Happy Birthday" to her. She felt overwhelmed.

Then, just when she thought it couldn't get better, Jonathan stood up and pulled a package from behind his back. "Mom," he said choking up, "Dad gave this to me the day before he died and told me to give it to you on Christmas Day. It's your birthday and Christmas gift from him."

Anna, with all that had happened in the past few weeks couldn't believe that anything more could surprise her.

Chapter 25

She opened it to find a beautiful white gold locket on a chain. Its heart-shape was engraved "Anna & Jerry" on one side and "Mercer 2009" on the other. She could hardly breathe as she opened it to reveal a portrait of a family – *Her Family*–including Trevor on one side and an old weathered picture of her and Jerry on the other.

This final gift from Jerry came, of course, wrapped in a paper bag.

CPSIA information can be obtained at www.ICGtesting.com
Printed in the USA
LVOW08s0740160414

381842LV00001B/7/P